THE OTTO DIGMORE
DIFFERENCE

BRENT HARTINGER

BOOKS

BK Books
www.brenthartinger.com

Cover design by Philip Malaczewski

ISBN-13: 978-1542810333

For Michael Jensen

And for all who are different.
Our differences are our strengths,
as individuals and as a society,
now more than ever.

CHAPTER ONE

People are staring at me, and I'm in the moment, and I want it to go on forever.

I'm boarding a plane in Seattle, and even the other First Class passengers have their eyes on me as I store my bag above my seat. One women is staring so intently her dangly earrings don't move, and I'm glad I wore my Vince V-neck because I like the way it makes my chest look.

The first person to actually talk to me is a teenage girl who's managed to work her way up from the aisle of Business Class.

"Sorry," she says. "Are you Otto Digmore?"

"I am," I say with my practiced modesty.

She holds up her phone, a bit meekly, meaning she wants to take a selfie with me.

"Sure thing," I say, cool and confident.

She steps toward my left side—they always step to my left side, at least if they have any say in the matter, as far from my right side as possible. I'm still not sure if it's because they're afraid to get too close to the right side of my face, or if they think it'll make a better photo if it isn't covered up.

The girl and I lean in close—her shampoo smells fruity, like fake strawberries—and out of the corner of my eye, I see her face suddenly light up like a Christmas tree, sparkling. I smile too, but more like cool neon, and she snaps the picture. I wait for her to check the screen, then smile apologetically and lean in for a second shot—they *always* want a second shot—and I smile again, exactly the same as before. By this point, the flight attendant has appeared, and she's all business, directing the girl back to her seat, then standing between me and the aisle, because she knows this could start a chain reaction and lots of other people will want selfies too, unless she puts a stop to it right now.

With the girl gone, I squeeze past a businessman in the aisle seat—he has white hair but actually looks kind of boyish—and I sit down next to the window.

"Can I get you both a drink before takeoff?" the flight attendant asks.

"I'll have a martini," the businessman says, but he's staring at me. I know it's partly because he's recognized me, knows that I'm famous, but he wouldn't be able to say why.

"Bottled water, please," I say.

Before she leaves, the flight attendant leans in and whispers to me conspiratorially, "You're the best part of *Hammered*."

The businessman grins: he's realized I'm an actor on a TV show. Finally, he has an explanation for his recognizing me, and for the girl wanting to take that selfie.

"Thanks," I say to the flight attendant, "that's so nice of you to say."

Hammered is a sitcom on the CW network, about this guy named Mike Hammer and all his friends in a college dorm—mostly about how they're always getting drunk and getting laid.

I play Dustin, one of the other guys in the dorm, even though I'm actually twenty-six years old. It's a supporting role, but I am a regular cast member, not just featured. The show debuted in June, and me and my character ended up getting a lot of attention. I even got invited to be on both *Stephen Colbert* and *Jimmy Kimmel*—the last guest slot on both, true, but I was the only actor from *Hammered* who was asked. It's the start of October now, and my life has been turned upside down. Somehow I've become a celebrity. And people stare at celebrities, and ask to take selfies, and generally make a big fuss.

It's taken a while to get used to being famous—to being the center of attention. The publicists at the studio all said the same thing: You're an actor, so think of being famous as a role you're playing. You're playing the version of "you" that your fans most want to see, someone humble and charming and accessible, and also cool and confident and hip. Your fans want to *like* you, so give them lots of reasons to do that.

This was good advice. And so for the last four months, I've been playing two roles: Dustin, my role on *Hammered*, and Otto Digmore, the celebrity I want everyone to like. As an actor, I know that the most important part of acting is about being present, being in the moment, or at least *seeming* that way, even if you're not necessarily feeling it.

Being famous is the strangest role I've ever played.

But being on *Hammered*, and being famous, isn't the reason I'm feeling so good right now.

I've just come from the weekend wedding of my friend Russel Middlebrook to his longtime boyfriend, Kevin Land. I wasn't in a very good mood when I got there—the reason why is a long story—and I hadn't expected to have a very good time. But it was amazing. I even sang a song I wrote for the occasion, and it went over really well.

The wedding was earlier today—it's evening now—and I'm still on a high. So right now it's easy to give off the sense of being humble and charming and accessible, and also cool and confident and hip. I barely have to act.

"Going to L.A., huh?" the boyish businessman with white hair asks me, and I'm aware it's a stupid question—we're on a plane to Los Angeles, obviously. But I smile and nod, because I know it's an excuse for him to talk to me, to tell his friends and maybe his kids that he spoke to Otto Digmore, an actual celebrity.

I turn and look out the window, but the lights are still on inside the plane, so all I see is the reflection of the First Class cabin in the clear plastic.

I also see my face—the whole right side.

It's covered with scars. In some places, it looks a little bit like my face is melting.

This is the *other* reason the businessman was staring at me. The good news is that I still have both my eyebrows.

I have more scars too. They run down onto my shoulder and chest, hidden by my clothes, and also up under my hairline. Most of my hair is real, but one small part of it isn't—it's a hairpiece that's woven into my actual hair. It was really expensive, and it has to be adjusted every three weeks, but it looks real. Not even my friend Russel knows about it.

4

When I was seven years old, I had an accident with some fire. I tell people I was playing with matches and some gasoline I found in the garage. I've never told anyone the truth, not even my parents or the therapist. I wanted to be Pyro, the X-Man who can control fire. I wasn't quite stupid enough to pour gasoline on myself, but I poured it on these Nerf sponge balls that I was going to light and throw. Didn't quite work out that way.

I know I was in a lot of pain for a long time, but I don't remember any of that. I guess I've blocked it out. There isn't any pain now, and I don't even notice if my skin is tight or anything—it just feels like me. But I have to be careful, because the smell of gasoline can still sometimes set off a panic attack.

My scars used to be worse. As I got older, I had surgeries and skin grafts, and the scars also healed more than any doctor ever told me they would. But it's impossible not to see them. If you touch them, they feel both smoother than other skin, and also thicker. Whiskers don't grow there, so I also have to shave every day, otherwise I look like I only have half a beard. That's probably the least of my worries, looks-wise, but it still makes me feel self-conscious.

Sitting in my window seat, I hear a scraping out on the tarmac, and I lean forward to look outside. I still can't see anything, only my own reflection in the plastic, but now I see the other side of my face, which looks like everyone else's—no scars. It's not like there's a clear dividing line between the two halves of my face, but if you only see me from the left, you can't see the scars at all.

I know it's weird that someone like me chose to become an actor, but it's what I've really wanted to do ever since high school. It's ironic that people stared at me even before I was a celebrity. They've stared at me for as long as I can remember. I could say that it's been really traumatizing, and it probably has been, but it's hard for me to know for sure, because that feels like me too. How people treated me before the accident is another thing I don't remember.

But the *way* people stare at me is definitely different now. Before, I could always feel the pity. Now it's mostly people with smiles on their faces and admiration in their eyes. Because I'm on TV. I'm one of the cool kids. That's never been me before.

"Here you go," the flight attendant says, putting my bottled water on the beverage holder on the armrest and giving the martini to the businessman. "Can I get you gentlemen anything else?"

"Nah, I'm good," I say, and I realize that the businessman is looking at me, leaning forward a half inch or so, trying to get a better look at the scarred side of my face.

I unscrew the top of my bottled water and lift it in sort of a "Cheers!" motion. The businessman joins me, smiling awkwardly, and we both drink.

It's strange to think that a big part of the reason I'm a celebrity now is *because* of my scars. It was sort of a fluke that the producers hired me. My agent somehow managed to get me an audition, and the producers liked me so much that they ended up creating a whole new character for me, basing him on my own experiences, writing my facial scars into the storylines. Then me and my character started getting all this attention. I stand out because I'm so different. That's ironic too, because I've been acting forever, but for a long time I couldn't get any parts at all, except as zombies in student films, and as the Elephant Man and the Phantom in *The Phantom of the Opera* in college productions.

Who would have thought that burning myself with gasoline when I was seven would have turned out to be a pretty good career move? But it did kind of work.

Almost everyone in the plane is seated now, and they're getting ready for takeoff. We'll be in the air soon with all our media devices turned off, but I decide to text Spencer, this guy I've gone out with a few times.

Sup? I write. **I had a great time at the wedding, but I really missed you!**

"Can I take a picture?" a voice says.

I look over, and it's a kid in the aisle, maybe ten years old, holding up his phone.

I glance at the businessman, apologizing with my eyes, but he's more impressed than anything. I also look around for the flight attendant, but she must be up in the galley pouring more drinks.

So I say to the kid, "Sure thing," cool and confident again. Then I squeeze my way back out into the aisle.

When the plane finally lands in Los Angeles and we can turn our phones on again, I immediately check to see if Spencer has texted me back. He hasn't. The flight between Seattle and L.A. is a little over two hours, and it seems weird that I still haven't heard from him, but I figure he's probably busy.

When I get to the baggage claim, someone asks for my autograph, which still always catches me a little by surprise. But I guess that's what people asked celebrities for before cellphones, before everyone wanted a selfie.

Somewhere in the background of the luggage claim, a teenage boy yells, "Freak!" and it echoes up into the cavernous space overhead. I pretend like I don't hear it, because it's a little like people asking for autographs—a reminder of how things used to be, but not something I have to concern myself with much anymore.

In the cab ride home from the airport, I check Twitter and Instagram and Facebook, and I see that people have posted all kinds of things, and sent me all these messages.

BURN BABY BURN! one says.

Someone else has posted a GIF of a chicken going into a deep-fat fryer.

And one person tells me, *Oh my GOD you're UGLY!!! WHY DON'T YOU KILL YOURSELF!!!*

The cab jerks to one side, then back again, and it feels a little bit like I'm being beat up by the words on my phone. People don't call me "Freak!" to my face much anymore, but they sure do online.

I said earlier that it was a long story about why I'd been feeling so bad before Russel and Kevin's wedding. This is the story: people have been harassing me online ever since *Hammered* debuted in June.

I guess it's not such a long story.

I know it's mostly the same people over and over. I recognize certain phrases, and the way they say things. Of course I block and report them, but it doesn't matter. They always come back with new profiles and new handles. It's like they've made it their mission in life to make me feel bad.

It's fun to be stared at on airplanes, to have people want to take selfies with me, and to finally feel like one of the cool kids. But there's a dark side to fame, especially for someone like me. You tell yourself it's the

Internet, that it's not real, which is kind of true. But I've still never felt anything like it, not even back in middle school.

Now I don't feel quite so high anymore. I'm having a hard time focusing, staying in the moment. Frankly I'm getting tired of being "on," of playing the part of Otto Digmore, Celebrity.

At the same time, I know I'll be home soon, and then I'll finally be able to relax.

It's after ten when the cab drops me off in front of my apartment building. It's dark now, and there isn't anyone else around on the whole block, but I can hear the growl of the city and feel the thrum of the nearby freeway in the concrete of the sidewalk under my feet.

I live in a pretty nice apartment building in Studio City, not too far from Warner Brothers, where they film *Hammered*. It's right off Ventura, and I have a view of the Valley and everything.

Before *Hammered*, I lived in this place called the Hive—this big old house in Fairfax with a bunch of struggling writers and actors. It was pretty great because there was always something exciting happening—someone playing music or rehearsing a play. I would have been fine staying there even after getting the show, especially since I spend most of my time on the set anyway.

But my agent Fiona Lang said that wouldn't look right, especially once I started doing press and journalists started profiling me. I didn't have time to get my own place, so my agent called up this real estate agent, who showed me three different apartments, and I picked one. The real estate agent had even arranged for an interior decorator to come in and furnish it all. As for all my old stuff, Fiona had said, "Forget it," even though she'd never even seen it.

Inside the building, I ride the elevator up to my apartment, staring at my blurred reflection in the stainless steel. Then I remember Spencer, and I check again to see if he's texted me back, but he hasn't. I can't resist checking his Facebook profile to see if he's online, and he is. So it's not like he's somewhere where he doesn't have access to his phone.

Is he ghosting me? I've heard people talk about that, but it's never happened to me before, mostly because I haven't dated a lot of guys. Only six, if you count all the guys I went out with more than once. And one was my friend Russel way back in high school, one is Spencer, and one was only two dates.

If Spencer *is* ghosting me, I'm weirdly intrigued, like I'm finally having an experience that everyone else had a long time ago, like I'm no longer a virgin. But mostly I feel bad. Will I ever see him again? "Ghosting" is the perfect term for it, because it'll be like he faded out of my life, but he won't ever be gone completely. I'll wonder what happened. It's a little bit like the people who are harassing me online: I can't see them either, and I'm not quite sure if they're real, but at the same time I can't forget about them.

The elevator door rolls open, and I step out into the hallway, which is painted dark purple with brown trim, and lit with dim mood lighting from recessed fixtures. Everything is spotless, and it smells like new carpet, but it feels strange too, how deserted it is.

As I approach the door to my unit, I see something white dripping down the dark wood of the door, like spilled milk. It almost glows. Did something leak—some chemical or something?

Moving closer, I realize it's something solid: white candle wax splattered against the wood, then hardened. There's a lot of it, some of it even down on the carpet. It looks like the blood of a robot in some futuristic movie.

I know instantly what this is all about, that it has to do with my face. All my life, people have said it looks like my face is melting, like wax on a candle.

Someone is harassing me in real life now, not just online.

I feel like a fly stuck to flypaper, like I'm trapped. Somehow I know that if I tell anyone about this, like the apartment manager or the police, they won't believe me, or they'll at least be skeptical. They'll think: "Maybe someone just spilled wax on the door. It's not like *everything* has to do with those scars on his face."

I stand there, still frozen. I'm definitely not breathing. Candle wax hardens fast, so I have no idea how long it's been since the person did this. Maybe they're even still in the building, down around the corner of the hallway. But I don't want to touch the wax either, to see if it's still warm.

I dig for my key, unlock the door, and stumble into my apartment.

I flick the light switch on even as something crinkles underneath me—a piece of paper on the floor. Someone must have slid it under the door.

I can see it from where I stand, a print-out of a photograph of a completely blackened body lying in some tall grass at night.

It's a gruesome picture, and an off-the-charts horrible thing to do to someone like me. Some part of me thinks: Well, now if I show the manager or the police the wax on my door, they won't immediately assume it was a harmless accident.

But it doesn't make me feel any better. It makes me feel *worse*. It's bad enough that they came to the *door* of my apartment—they also sort of got inside. It's one thing to be harassed online, which feels real enough, but this is *really* real. Whoever did it also knows where I live, and I can't help but wonder if they'll be back. Or maybe it was someone in my apartment building who did this, someone who wants me to move out. I'm suddenly not sure which is scarier.

Without thinking, I reach down and snatch the paper, crumpling it into a tight ball.

This doesn't make me feel any better either. I actually feel a little bit like an idiot, because if I do decide to call the police, I've now tampered with the evidence.

"Is everything okay?"

It's the neighbor from down the hall, right outside my door, and her voice makes me jump in surprise.

"Oh," she says, seeing she startled me. "I didn't mean to scare you."

I've seen her in the hallway before, and we've always said hi. She's in her early forties, with unnaturally shiny chestnut hair and perfect skin. I think she's a publicist at one of the studios.

She's looking down at the wax splattered on my door, concern on her face.

"No," I say, "I'm fine." I nod to the wax. "Some kid, I guess."

"Some kid?" she says, surprisingly blunt. "Who?"

"I don't know." I consider asking her when she first saw the wax, if she has any idea when it happened, but somehow I don't have the energy.

"Someone who lives in the building? Or did someone else get inside? This is vandalism, you know." The panic rises in her voice.

"Yeah," I say, overwhelmed by her energy. At this point, I'm glad I haven't shown her the print-out of the photograph.

"You need to call someone," she goes on. "The manager, for sure. And also the police. Should I call the police right now?"

She's already fumbling in a pocket for her phone, but the last thing in the world I want to do is talk to the police.

"No, it's okay," I say, but she doesn't stop digging for her phone. "*Really.*"

She glances up at me, a little stunned.

"Look," she says, "you're Otto Digmore, right? The actor?"

"Yeah," I say, but at this moment in time, it seems impossible to play the role of Otto Digmore, Celebrity, for even one second more.

"I think we need to take this seriously," she says, "if your fans are somehow getting inside our building to pull these kinds of pranks..."

"I'm really sorry," I say, "but I just got home from a trip, and I'm exhausted."

"But—"

I close the door in her face. Then I lock and bolt it, even though I know she can hear me, and probably thinks it's some kind of hostile gesture.

Alone again, I turn and face my apartment.

It's spotless, even cleaner than the hallway outside. In earlier times in my life when I've gone away on a trip, I've come home to my house or apartment, and I can smell how it really smells, the scent I'd gotten used to before and didn't notice. But I don't smell anything now, just the vague scent of disinfectant. I have a maid service, but that's not why things are the way they are. It's because I've spent so little time here since I moved in. I've spent most of the last seven months at the studio, filming episodes of *Hammered*, and I mostly only come home to sleep. When was the last time I cooked a meal here? Have any of my friends ever visited?

I shuffle deeper into the apartment. I look around the front room, at the white lamps and black leather couch, at the black throw rug, the framed black-and-white photos on the walls. Everything is tasteful and coordinated, but it feels like the staging at an open house. I'd been looking forward to coming home, to having some time to myself after the chaos of the weekend and the last few months, but this doesn't feel like home. Why would it? There's nothing here I chose. I paid for everything, but it's a reflection of my interior designer's taste, not mine. It was all done to fool entertainment journalists into thinking I'm someone I'm not.

I head into the bedroom and drop my overnight bag on the floor. But then I just stand there, not even turning on the light.

Only a few hours before, I felt so good, completely on a high, totally in the moment, but I don't feel that way now. I can't focus. I have no idea where to turn, what to do next, even what to feel.

People have told me that Otto Digmore, Celebrity, is another role I'm supposed to play, but now I see that Otto Digmore, Me, is a role too, but one I'm playing very badly. I've forgotten my lines, and I don't know my blocking, where my marks are. I'm definitely not in the moment—I'm completely out of character.

This is all so ironic. I'm a TV star now, a celebrity. I'm rich and famous, all my dreams are coming true. But I'm already tired of the dark side of fame, being harassed and hated—first online, now even here at my lonely apartment I never see, full of stuff I didn't buy.

Hey, just because something is ironic, that doesn't mean it isn't true.

CHAPTER TWO

I feel better when I wake up the next morning. Things seem brighter even in the smoggy, hazy light of a new day in Los Angeles.

The first thing I do, before breakfast, is take some photos of the wax on my front door. Then I start to pick at it, and the blotches and streaks all snap right off, and that's incredibly satisfying. Next I scrape the wax out of the carpet with a butter knife, and do that trick where you iron a brown paper bag, and the melted wax soaks up into the paper. When I'm done, you can't tell it was ever there, not unless you get down and touch the carpet itself, which still feels gummy.

This makes me feel even better, like I have some power over the situation, and maybe also over my whole life. I decide not to call the police, but I do email the photos to the apartment manager.

But Spencer still hasn't texted me back, so I accept the fact that I have officially been ghosted.

Finally, I have breakfast—cut pineapple and dry cereal, since I'm out of milk—but as I'm eating, I realize I have another problem: I have nothing to do.

I've been insanely busy for months, ever since *Hammered* got its series order back in February. It was partly the filming itself. *Hammered* is a single-camera show, which means each episode is filmed like a little twenty-two-minute movie, not before a live audience. And that means lots of different takes and angles and close-ups, and more locations than a live audience show. As a supporting player, not a lead, I spend most of my time sitting around waiting, with only a few lines and close-ups. But because there are so many group scenes, I still have to be available a lot.

Hammered also involves a lot of publicity: interviews, going to charity events, sucking up to the executives at the different affiliates. I'm pretty sure I ended up doing more publicity even than Arvin Mason, the guy who plays Mike Hammer—the actual star of the whole show.

But *Hammered* went into hiatus the month before. That means we'd finished filming all fifteen episodes of the first season, and now we have a break for a couple of months before we go back to film a second season—*if* we film a second season. *Hammered's* ratings are okay, not great, and the reviews were mostly bad—a 32 on Metacritic and 4.8 on IMDb, which both stink—even though I personally got a lot of good notices.

Ever since the start of the hiatus, I've kept busy, finishing up the last of my commitments for *Hammered*, doing pick-ups and ADR, but also getting ready for Russel's wedding, writing that song for him and doing some other stuff for the bachelor party.

But this Monday morning, today, for the first time since I can't remember, I finally have nothing to do.

I thought that would be relaxing after so many months of non-stop work, but it isn't. It's actually sort of discombobulating. After having your life so heavily scheduled for so long, it's strange to not have any structure at all. It's like trying to play a role with no script, and not even any other actors to improvise with.

I think about the other people in the cast of *Hammered*—Bryan and Elliott and Regina and Arvin Mason. We'd all gotten pretty close these past few months, spending all that time together on the set, having M&M fights and playing hide-and-seek in our dressing rooms. I consider texting one of them, maybe even Arvin, although I always got the sense that he didn't like me, mostly because I ended up getting more publicity than he did even though he was the star of the show.

But somehow it feels strange. For one thing, I wonder if they aren't sick of me, the way I'm kind of sick of them. Are we even "friends"? It was more like we were soldiers that had all been assigned on a nuclear submarine together for the last seven months. So why in the world would we want to spend more time together now? Over the summer, I'd also met lots of other celebrities, people like Zachary Quinto, who had once even set me up on a blind date. But those interactions always felt so situational—I know they were mostly being polite—so they now feel even less like friends than the cast members from *Hammered*.

I think about my friends from before I got cast on a TV show, like my ex-housemates from the Hive. But then I remember how I'd gone to visit them once after I'd gotten the show, and it had been really awkward. Half of them were jealous, and the other half thought I'd sold out by doing such a stupid, mainstream show.

Finally, I remember my old friend Russel. But then I realize how he probably isn't even back in Los Angeles yet, and just got married anyway.

So I decide to hang out by myself. First, I go to the gym. Then I try catching up on all the things I hadn't been able to do over the summer. I play Pokémon Go, which is fun, but not blow-my-mind fun. Next I order a pizza, then start in on all the television I haven't had time to watch, including this show, *Stranger Things*, that everyone's been going crazy for. It's really good, and I can't help but feel jealous, because it's so obviously a lot better than *Hammered*.

Basically, I spend the whole week working out, then pigging out and vegging out. In the process, I make the apartment as messy and chaotic as I can. I didn't buy any of the furnishings, didn't choose any of the art, but now I'm doing my best to make my apartment look— and smell—as lived in as possible.

It doesn't really work, but at least no one comes back and slides anything horrible under my door.

Some part of me thinks it's only a matter of time before they do.

That Friday afternoon, I get a call from Greg, my agent Fiona's assistant.

"Can you come in and see us on Monday?" Greg says.

"Sure thing," I say. "What's up?"

"Fiona just wants to talk. She says there's lots to go over."

I have a feeling she has bad news, probably about *Hammered*, because good news almost always requires a quick answer, which means it comes over the phone. And if she does have bad news for me, she probably wants to console me, to let me down gently.

On the other hand, there's more to my career than *Hammered*, and I've been wanting to have a talk with Fiona about what comes next. And after a week of rest, I'm finally ready to think about that.

Fiona has been my agent for a long time. Actors talk about "choosing" their agent, but the truth is that it's really hard to get a legitimate agent to represent you, at least when you're a nobody. So when you're first starting out, you pretty much take whoever you can get.

When I met Fiona, my career was going nowhere, though I had gotten pretty good at playing a zombie in all those student films. I'd talked to a ton of other agents and managers, auditioning for them in their offices and in various showcase productions around town.

All those other agents rejected me and never said why. Maybe it wasn't my scars. Plenty of other actors were rejected too, even some of the ones with looks and talent.

Finally, Fiona came up to me after one of the showcases and said, "You're good. And with that face, you'd be an interesting challenge."

She's not with one of the big agencies—CAA or United or William Morris. She has her own boutique agency, just her and her assistant, but she knows her stuff. And the fact is, she did get me the job on *Hammered*. It's funny because the instant my sitcom got picked up, I immediately heard from all these other agents, including people at those bigger agencies. A couple of them had rejected me before, even if they didn't remember. But now that I had a part on a net-work sitcom, suddenly they wanted me. They all said I was making a big, big mistake staying with a nobody agent like Fiona, who couldn't do any packaging. That's when agencies put projects together themselves, mostly using their own clients. But I wasn't about to leave Fiona, and not just because I felt a lot of loyalty. What did it say about these other agents that they only wanted me on the way up?

So Monday morning, I hop in my blue Mini-Cooper Convertible, and head over to Beverly Hills to meet with Fiona. I bought the car not long after *Hammered* was picked up, but for once, it wasn't because someone told me to, or because I was trying to impress a reporter.

Hey, I liked it.

Fiona's office isn't that far from some of the big agencies, but it's on a side street, in a little triangular building, wedged into a sharp corner. I asked her about it once, and she said, "The only point of those big, flashy buildings is to impress their clients. You want me to impress you, I'll buy you some chocolates. Otherwise, let me do my damn job."

Fiona is nothing if not practical. Which is another reason why I like her.

That Monday afternoon, I'm walking up to her office, girding myself, because I'm still expecting bad news.

Inside her waiting room, I find Greg, her assistant, sitting at his desk. He's this Native guy, big and tall, with a ponytail and a Los Angeles Rams jersey. Greg is another way Fiona isn't like most other agents, because most of their assistants all look exactly the same, in pressed white shirts flashing creepy robot smiles.

"You're here!" he says, beaming. For some reason, it doesn't seem like a big guy like Greg should be giddy, but he usually is—today maybe even more than usual.

"How are you?" I say.

"*People Magazine* says they might put you on their next list of the One Hundred Most Beautiful People!" he blurts, like a little kid unable to keep a secret.

It takes a second to make sense of what he's told me.

"It's true!" he says. "Isn't that great?"

Even now, I'm tempted to say, "You're joking, right?" But the more I think about it, the more it kind of makes sense. I really have been getting a lot of publicity lately—and *People* already did a full-page profile on me. Obviously, they don't really think I'm beautiful: if people really thought that, I would have dated more than six guys in my life. But I'm one of their make-a-point picks, like when they chose dark-skinned Lupita Nyong'o, or transgender Laverne Cox, or Jane Fonda at age seventy-six. Except, unlike me, those other people really *are* beautiful. The whole point is to pick someone unexpected, to say to the world, "Our standards of beauty are too narrow!"

Which I absolutely agree with. But I am still having a hard time processing this whole me-as-one-of-the-World's-Most-Beautiful-People thing. I appreciate the thought, but what's the cost? Are people going to laugh at me—at the whole idea of me being beautiful? Well, *obviously* people are going to laugh at me, because they already are. But are they going to do it *more*?

Finally, I think: Who cares? Hells to the yes, I'll be one of the World's Most Beautiful People. Even if it *is* a make-a-point pick, and even if people do make fun of me on social media. The better news is that this meeting with Fiona isn't what I thought it was at all—a way for her to give me bad news in person in order to console me and let me down gently.

"When?" I say.

"Spring," he says. "They'll let us know in February."

Right then I notice a tattoo on Greg's tan bicep, partly under his sleeve—something I don't remember seeing before. At first I think it's a feather, but then I realize it's a salmon swimming upstream. I don't have any tattoos because I figure enough of my skin is different as it is. But I admit I'm always curious: Why exactly would a person deliberately choose to mark their skin?

I'm about to ask about the tattoo when another voice says, "Otto?"

It's Fiona, standing in the doorway of her office. She's an Asian woman, sixtyish, on the small side, but with big, blocky jewelry.

"Come in," she says, withdrawing inside like a snail disappearing into its shell. "We'll talk."

As I head for the door, Greg gives me a big, goofy two-thumbs-up.

But the second I'm inside Fiona's office and the door is closed, she says, "You're canceled."

Once again, it takes a second for the words to make sense.

"*Hammered*," she goes on. "They're not doing a second season. I found out on Friday, but I didn't want to tell you over the phone. There's one more episode to air, then they're announcing it to the press."

So I was right before: this *is* a "bad news" meeting.

"Sit," she says, nodding to the chair, and I do. She sits too. The building is triangular, and Fiona's office is in the tip of the triangle. Her desk is backed up against the point of the tip, so she faces out at me like she's speaking from inside a megaphone.

On her desk, I see a half-open script, and I wonder if it's something she was reading for me.

"Well," I say, "there's still the Most Beautiful Person thing. Greg told me. That's pretty great news, isn't it?"

She slumps in her chair a little, not unlike a toad. "I wouldn't get too excited about that. Five months is a long time in Hollywood. Things change."

So much for Fiona consoling me, letting me down gently. That's when I remember that Fiona never really beats around the bush—that she's sometimes a little *too* practical.

"You have some heat right now," Fiona goes on. "We need to capitalize on that, get you into another high-profile project. *Hammered* being canceled is a set-back, but it's also an opportunity. Speaking of which, you're still not planning on coming out, right?"

"No," I say with a sigh.

This is something that Fiona and I talked about before I made it big, whether or not I should come out publicly as gay. At first the whole conversation felt wrong: there isn't anything wrong with being gay, and it isn't anything to be ashamed of. But Fiona had explained that from a "career" perspective, my being openly gay would make a difference. Having facial scars was one thing—a *big* thing—but being openly gay was an entirely different thing. Even now, a lot of producers and casting directors worry about casting out gay actors in non-gay roles. They always insist they're not homophobic, but they worry that audiences might be, at least in the South and other parts of the world, and they can't afford to take that chance. According to Fiona, I'm already limited in the roles I can try out for because of the scars on my face. Why make things even more difficult by giving casting directors yet another reason not to hire me?

But here's the funny thing: in all the interviews I've done for *Hammered*, all the press events and red carpets, no one has ever asked me about my personal life, if I was seeing anyone. Not one single time. This is even stranger when you consider that that's *all* interviewers ever want to know about the other young, hot members of the *Hammered* cast: "Who are you dating?" "What do you say about the rumors that you're gay?" No reporter ever asked me anything like that, because it was like people couldn't even *conceive* of the idea that I'd be in a relationship, that anyone would ever want to have sex with me. This is what I mean when I say that *People* Magazine maybe picking me as one of the 100 Most Beautiful People is clearly them trying to make a point.

At least that's one thing I don't have to worry about online, that I'll ever be outed. People don't care whether non-sexual or unattractive people are gay. So if I ever do come out, I'll definitely need to force the issue.

"That's good," Fiona says, nodding. "Because we have a really interesting offer on the table. I think we're finally going to get you into feature films."

I straighten in my chair. Feature films? So this is a "good news" meeting after all. My head is spinning, with everything going back and forth like this. But after being ghosted by Spencer, harassed online and off, and having my sitcom canceled, I'm pretty sure I deserve a little good news.

"New Line is re-rebooting *A Nightmare on Elm Street*," Fiona says.

I sit there like a statue, afraid to move or I'll crack into a hundred pieces. I know exactly what Fiona is going to say next:

They want me to read for Freddy Krueger.

"And they want you to read for Freddy Krueger!" Fiona says, a huge, phony smile on her face.

I knew she was going to say it, but I still can't quite believe it when she does. An actual burn survivor playing Freddy Krueger, a scary villain with burns all over his face? And, of course, it would be the first major film to feature an actual burn survivor in a leading role— seri-ously, I've looked this up—and he would be this hor-rible monster who terrorizes kids in their dreams. I'm not necessarily against the idea of *ever* playing a villain, but hopefully not for my first role in a feature film, and not in yet another role that completely reinforces the idea that "burn survivor" equals "scary" and "evil," like *A Nightmare on Elm Street* and a zillion other movies totally do.

I know that Fiona can read on my face what I'm thinking. She obviously knew all along how I'd react, and she was playing me, trying to gently lead me down some kind of primrose path.

"Now wait!" she says. "Before you say anything, just listen. They want to do this really interesting thing where they recreate your face using CGI for the first part of the film, before you're burned."

I still don't talk, or even move. This is offensive too. Does she really think this is going to make me *more* likely to take the part?

Fiona stares at me, but now I'm not sure what she's thinking. The stones in her big blocky bracelet clink.

"Okay, okay," Fiona says at last. "But before we reject it, keep in mind that I think I can get you a million bucks. Maybe a million and a half."

A million and a half bucks? This is so unexpected that it takes my breath away for a second.

But I know I can't take the role. It's a hell of a lot of money, but it's not enough to make up for the fact that it wouldn't only be random people harassing me after that. Actual burn survivors would probably show up outside my apartment, trying to set my building on fire and burn me all over again.

Hey, I can make jokes like that, but other people can't.

"What else do you have?" I ask.

"Honestly?" she says. "That's the least offensive offer of all. There's a post-apocalyptic thriller about a guy with a burned face, but he ends up being the villain, and the second half is all about how scary the guy is. Plus, it's an indie so the pay is shit. And there are about six zombie films. For some reason, everyone think it's *hilarious* casting you as a zombie."

This shouldn't surprise me because I've played a lot of zombies in my career, but it does. For some reason, I'd assumed that my success on *Hammered* would have changed things, at least a little.

"I've also gotten an offer for some stage work," Fiona says.

"Let me guess," I say. "The Elephant Man or the Phantom in *The Phantom of the Opera.*"

"Actually, it's the Child Catcher in *Chitty Chitty Bang Bang.*"

At least casting directors are thinking of me now, which isn't something that every actor in Hollywood can say. On the other hand, they're only thinking of me when they cast ugly, child-terrorizing monsters.

"I'd say consider it," Fiona goes on, "but it's a national tour, not Broadway, and the pay is shit too."

I inhale, trying to steady myself. It really is like Fiona is speaking from within a megaphone, because what she's saying is coming through loud and clear.

"Well, it's almost pilot season," I say at last. "At least I can read for some of the new shows."

Fiona nods, but once again I can tell there's something she's not telling me.

"What?" I say. She doesn't answer, so I say, "Come on, you can tell me. I can take it."

"Well, I've been calling around on that too, but everyone says it's too late to do any rewriting. And they *all* say you would take rewriting. I try to talk about the promotional value in your casting, but they all seem to think that juice has been squeezed."

I'd said I could take it, but now I'm not sure I can. It's strange having my entire existence reduced to a gimmick, and then being told the gimmick is old hat.

"So the movie and theater offers all suck," I say. "And no one's willing to read me for a pilot. What do I do?"

"Well, we just have to wait," she says. "Maybe something will turn up."

In the past, Fiona has told me the same thing over and over: that I'm really, really talented, and it's only a matter of time before people see that. And also that society is changing fast, and things that were so strange a few years earlier—transgender characters who aren't just punchlines or hookers! disabled characters played by actual disabled actors!—aren't so strange anymore.

I'm waiting for her to say it now, but she doesn't. Which is ironic because, by any measure at all, my career is more successful than it's ever been. Does Fiona think that's all in the past? Does *she* think the juice has been squeezed too?

Her jewelry clinks again, and somehow I sense her impatience—with this meeting, and also with me. She eyes that half-open script, and somehow I know it's a project for one of her other clients, not me. In other words, she's said everything she wanted to say, and the meeting is over.

I stand and turn. "Well..."

Fiona clears her throat and I look back her.

"You're absolutely sure about Freddy Krueger?" she says. "I mean, I could always ask for two million just to see what they say. And if we could tell *People* we booked you a feature, that would almost guarantee the Most Beautiful People thing."

This feels a little bit like being tempted by the Devil. There was a time when I probably would have done any role at all for a million bucks. On the other hand, I know now that if I took that role, it might be the last good one I'd ever get. So in this case, it's easy to tell the Devil to fuck off.

"I'm sure," I say.

Still, there is something about Fiona asking again that kind of bugs me. I know she's practical, and she's probably *being* practical even now. But does she really think this is the best I can do—and that this is the best thing for my career? I am twenty-six years old, I've been famous for a grand total of not even five months, and I'm already washed up? It doesn't quite seem possible. No boyfriend, no real friends, and now no career?

And yet somehow I know that all those people harassing me online, and now also in person, won't stop harassing me, no matter how far my career falls.

* * *

Out in the waiting room, Greg immediately looks up. "How'd it go?" he says.

"Not so great," I say. I briefly tell him what Fiona told me, but I assume he already knows. Assistants know everything, sometimes even more than the agents they work for.

As I talk, Greg furrows his brow. I try not to lay it on too thick, that I'm thinking I might already be washed up, after only a few months of fame. On the other hand, for the first time in my life, maybe I wouldn't mind a little pity.

When I'm done, Greg clenches his fists and says, "Can I just say? I so hate this town. The whole herd mentality. Everyone only wants what everyone else wants."

"Tell me about it."

"Nobody ever wants anything different, not unless they think everyone else wants it too, and that defeats the whole point."

"Tell me about that too."

"Well, I hope you're not too discouraged," he says. He lowers his voice. "I shouldn't say this, but out of all our clients, I think you're the most talented. Most of our other clients can't do what you do."

I blush. Living in Hollywood—where everyone is constantly obsessing over Nielsen ratings, box office grosses, and Q-ratings—it's pretty easy to forget that movies and TV also have something to do with actual acting ability. I like that Greg sees that in me.

"I know the roles are limited right now," Greg goes on, "but I think that's changing, I really do. *Hammered* was a nice start, but it didn't show what you can truly do. I have a feeling the right part for you is right around the corner."

Now I smile. This is exactly the kind of thing I'd wanted Fiona to say, what she always said before—what agents are *supposed* to say. But she hadn't said it.

"In fact..." he says.

There's something about his voice that makes me perk up a bit. "Yeah?"

"Well, it's a bit of a long shot, but I was reading this script, and I think it'd be perfect for you. It's called *The Tulip Vase.*"

"What's the part?"

"The lead," Greg says. "It'll take a little rewriting to make it work for you, but not that much. The character is in an earthquake toward the beginning of the movie. I figured, Why couldn't it be a fire? In fact, when you read the script, I think a fire actually makes more sense, and your scars make the ending make more sense too." He looks down at his desk. "Would you be okay with that?"

People have asked me this before, and it's a totally fair question: Would it be traumatizing for me to play a burn victim, especially if it meant portraying an actual fire?

"It's fine." I'm an actor through and through. Actors are always saying how their bodies are their instruments, which I kind of hate because it sounds so pretentious and self-important, but it's also true. My body is what it is, and I shouldn't have gone into acting if I'm not okay with that.

"Who's doing it?" I say.

"Fox," Greg says.

"A studio film?"

Greg nods. "It's a big deal. Julian Lockwood directing."

Julian Lockwood? I know he won an Oscar a few years before, and has been nominated at least one other time. He's a really big deal.

"They'd never cast me," I say. "I don't have enough feature credits."

"Well, we'd need to get them to buy into our vision," Greg says, "which involves rebranding you as a romantic lead. But you have a remarkable personal story, and I still don't think it's been fully cultivated."

I've never heard Greg talk like this—sound so professional. Before, he's always seemed a little like someone's badly dressed, over-eager kid brother, even though he's probably older than I am, in his mid-thirties. Or maybe I saw him that way because of the way he looks and dresses—not like other assistants.

I also really like what he's saying, that maybe all my juice *hasn't* been squeezed yet.

"The point is," Greg goes on, "I think we could at least get you an audition."

As I consider all this, I remember something. "Why didn't Fiona mention it?"

"She hasn't read it," Greg says. "It just came across my desk, and I haven't run it by her yet. But I immediately thought of you."

This is what I mean about assistants knowing more than their agents.

I'm suddenly excited about the part, even if I know it's a really long shot.

"Can you email it to me?" I say to Greg.

He smiles and hits a key on the keyboard of his computer, almost like it was all ready to go.

"Done," he says with a grin.

CHAPTER THREE

I'm really curious about *The Tulip Vase*. So I pay the meter outside Fiona's office, put the top down, and read it right there in the car.

I can see right away why it's a studio film, not a little indie one. It needs a big budget. It has an epic, larger-than-life vibe, like *Forrest Gump*.

It's the story of Zach and Maggie, who first meet in college. They're from the opposite side of the tracks, but when they meet, they have this instant connection. However, Zach has commitments and obligations, so he lets the moment pass him by. He regrets it almost immediately, but when he goes back to find Maggie, a freak earthquake hits. A valuable tulip vase falls off a table and shatters. Before Zach can find Maggie, he's injured and hospitalized—this is the point where there could instead be some kind of fire where Zach is burned, exactly like Greg said.

Months later, when Zach recovers, he tracks Maggie down, but by then she's moved on with someone else.

The rest of the script, their paths keep crossing, usually at big, dramatic events like 9/11, the election of Obama, and Hurricane Sandy. Zach and Maggie keep having these amazing connections, but something always keeps them from getting together—other lovers, career issues, security concerns.

The ending is especially good. Maggie has finally decided that there's no way she and Zach can ever be together, so she's marrying someone else. Zach tries one last time to win her over with this complicated plan to finally set everything right. It's a great plan, and you absolutely expect it to work, for everything to come together in a big, grand romantic climax—and everyone will get their happy ending.

But it's a disaster. Everything goes wrong: Zach is fired, Maggie is disinherited, an aging parent dies alone. Zach and Maggie have tried again and again to do the right thing, but it's never worked, and now they're surrounded by the unintended consequences of their doomed and tragic love, all this misery and resentment.

In the midst of all this tragedy, they both return to the place where they first met. It's all very understated, not triumphant at all, especially compared to the epic, sweeping feel of the rest of the movie. They smile that they both thought to come here, but they don't kiss. Maggie sees the vase that was broken at the beginning of the movie—someone has reassembled it. She fills it with water, then puts her wedding bouquet from the wedding into it, and she and Zach walk away, not holding hands even now. Still, in a way, love does sort of conquer all.

But the last shot of the movie is of the tulip vase, leaking water onto the bureau. It was put back together, but not perfectly. The vase is still broken.

So the ending is ambiguous. It says that life is messy and complicated, and sometimes there are no truly happy endings. The take-away is that we need to be brave and bold, and not let opportunities pass you by the first time around. Because if you do blow it, some mistakes can't be fixed.

Sitting in my car, I'm tearing up when I finish. It's mostly because it's such a beautiful script—big and cinematic, but also intimate and touching. It's definitely not your usual love story. I'm trying to think of the last time a studio script was this daring.

But I'm also crying because I can see how it's a great script for me. On one hand, it's not a "disability" script. It's not "about" the tragedy of having scars on my face, or any disability at all. But at the same time, my scars could truly inform the script, making it even better—more powerful. The whole point of the movie is that not all injuries heal completely. Sometimes you have to live with scars. And at the end of the script, Zach literally has a limp from the earthquake, and Maggie has lost some of her vision in an airplane crash. It would be easy, even better, to have Zach be burned instead. I'd even be willing to let them CGI my face for the scenes before any fire, like Fiona had said they wanted to do with the Freddy Krueger movie. That would be perfect too, and even though Greg didn't say it, I know it would make a great media angle, like how everyone talked about how they used CGI to make Brad Pitt look younger and younger in that movie, *The Curious Case of Benjamin Button.*

I call Fiona back, and Greg answers the phone.

"It's me," I say.

"You're sitting in your car outside, aren't you?" he says. "You read the script even before you went home."

"How did you know?"

"Because I've been watching you from the window."

"Oh," I say.

"I'm kidding!" Greg says. "I'm not watching—well, I did look once. But I knew you'd want to read it as fast as possible. And was I right, or was I right?"

"You were right." This is what I say, but what I'm thinking is: I really want this part. And: This could change absolutely everything about my career, forcing people to see me an entirely new way. And: I'll do whatever it takes to get cast.

Greg doesn't say anything on the other end of the phone, but I can tell he's smiling.

"Can I talk to Fiona?" I say.

"She's on another call, but I told her about the script, and she loves the idea. She's halfway through it right now."

"Do you think she can get me an audition?"

"Have you *met* Fiona? She flusters pit bulls. Give us some time, but we'll get back to you ASAP."

Part of me wants to wait in the car right outside Fiona's office, but that seems a little stalker-y. Besides, it could be days before I hear anything. And the answer might still be no.

So I drive home, and I'm pulling into the parking garage when my phone rings again.

It's Greg, and he says, "I've got good news and bad news."

But I don't want to play the whole "good news/bad news" game. I only want to know if Fiona got me an audition.

So I say that: "Do I have an audition?"

It seems like forever before he talks, but it probably isn't any time at all.

"Yes," he says. I can sense him smiling again on the other end of the phone.

For a second, I really am speechless. Could this really be happening? But I know it's way too soon to get excited.

"Do I really have a shot at this?" I ask.

"You really have a shot, Otto, I swear to you. They know who you are, and we explained our thinking, and they're excited to see you. They get it. Trust me, they know this movie is special."

I consider all this, and I decide that Greg is truly leveling with me. The one advantage of being with a smaller agency is that no studio movie would agree to read me unless they were really interested. It's not like CAA or United or William Morris, where they'd give me a courtesy read whether they were interested or not, to keep from pissing off the agent.

"They also know they need to get the casting absolutely right," Greg goes on. "And can I just say? I got the sense that they're not entirely happy with their current choices."

"*You* got the sense?"

"I may have been listening in on the call," Greg says, embarrassed.

At this, I can't help but wonder who I'm up against for the part. Arvin Mason, the star of *Hammered*? Part of me likes the idea of stealing his thunder one more time because he really has been kind of a dick to me all season long. But more likely it's Robert Pattinson, Kit Harrington, or Alex Pettyfer. Or maybe Liam Hemsworth or Nicholas Hoult. They're all actual movie stars, much bigger names than I am. But weirdly, none of these fresh-faced pretty boys scare me all that much, because I know they're not right for the part. Those are guys who all seem *destined* for happy endings. The ending of *The Tulip Vase* wouldn't work with someone like that.

Then I remember Miles Teller, who actually *would* be right for the part. He makes me nervous, because he's not such a pretty boy, and also because he has scars on his face too, even if they're a lot less noticeable than mine. Or maybe they would rewrite the movie for someone older, a superstar like Brad Pitt or Leonardo DiCaprio. If those guys were interested, they'd get the part whether they were right for it or not, because that's how Hollywood works.

I need to get a grip. Either I'm going to get the part, or I'm not, and no amount of stressing about it is going to make any difference.

"But...." Greg starts to say.

"What?" I say, thinking, Here comes the bad news.

"They're further along with casting than we thought," he says. "They need to make a final decision very soon."

"Which means?"

"Your audition is this afternoon. Or, more specifically, in one hour."

Of course I'm panicking. Having an audition in an hour means I don't have any time to prepare. I barely have time to get to Century City, the place where the audition is taking place.

"Otto, it's okay," Greg says, trying to talk me down off the ledge. "Relax. They *know* this is a cold reading. Mostly, they just want to meet you. Not having any time to prepare is a *good* thing, because it also means you don't have any time to freak yourself out."

I'm about to respond that this doesn't make any sense to me at all—that I could easily show up at the audition both absolutely unprepared and also completely freaked out.

But I don't have time to argue. I tell Greg to send me the address, and I start for Century City, even as I think about how long it's been since they adjusted my hairpiece, and what I'm wearing—one of my oldest shirts, but at least my loafers are Salvatore Ferragamo. I'm rethinking literally every choice I've made in the last twenty-four hours, including the fact that I had pizza with extra garlic the night before. At least I don't have any zits, which I realize is kind of an ironic thing for a guy with big scars on his face to worry about, but I *do* worry, because I still get them, and they always appear at exactly the wrong time.

It's not *that* far from Studio City to Century City, but it's not that close either, and it involves winding your way through the Hollywood Hills.

Right away, I run into traffic.

Traffic in Los Angeles isn't like traffic in other big cities: it's so much worse. Once you pull out of your driveway, it's like you're in the middle of a monster truck rally, and you're the guy in the clown car, especially if you're driving a Mini-Cooper Convertible.

At some point, I realize I'm never going to make it to the audition on time, so I call Greg, and he says, "It's okay, they know this was a last-minute thing. I'll call and let them know, but don't do anything stupid—just get there as fast as you can."

So I inch my car through the snarl of traffic, trying to burrow my way into Century City like a weevil. I end up parking in the wrong garage, but I'm pretty sure I'm only a couple of buildings away from where I need to be, so I park and run the rest of the way.

Now in addition to needing my hairpiece adjusted, wearing ratty clothes, and having garlic breath, I'm also sweaty and stinky. On the other hand, there may have been some truth to what Greg was saying about being in such a rush that I don't really have time to panic.

The lobby of the right building is airy and open—a lot nicer than the places where I usually audition. I check in with the receptionist, hoping I have time to freshen up in the restroom, but I'm already almost an hour late, so she immediately stands and says, "They're waiting for you. Right this way."

She leads me down a hallway and into a room, completely nondescript and empty except for a folding table and chairs directly across from me. There are three people at the table—two women and a man. There's also a man with a video camera on a tripod.

Everyone at the table looks over at me, and I have the feeling that I've interrupted something. I see they're all attractive with smooth skin and blindingly white teeth. The man at the camera fiddles with some dials. He's dark-skinned, probably Latino, and the only non-white person in the room.

"Hi," I say. "I'm Otto Digmore. And I'm so sorry I'm late!"

"It's totally fine," someone at the table says.

Then they all introduce themselves, but I don't step forward to shake their hands or anything because that's a huge faux pas for an actor in casting sessions. Today I'm actually glad we don't shake hands—it means they're less likely to smell the garlic on my breath. I do make a point to nod to the video operator, mostly because I try not to be a dick, but also because I'm aware it makes a good impression. I face the table again.

Something still feels off.

There's an actors' expression that says you can't get a part just by walking into a room, but you sure can lose it. That's because the people you're auditioning for always make a snap judgment the second they first see you: Do you look like how they see the character? And, for most leading roles, especially if you're female: Are you fuckable? If the answer to either of these questions is no, it really doesn't matter how good your audition is. And as an actor, you can always tell whether you pass this first test—if they're taking you seriously or not. Because of my scars, I'm pretty used to feeling like the producers have decided against me even as I'm walking into the room, at least if I'm auditioning for anything other than the disfigured monster who lives underneath the opera house.

But for the first time in my career, I have no idea what the people at that table are thinking. It doesn't feel like they've rejected me outright. Then again, they knew who I was before I came in, that I have scars on my face. At the same time, there's some kind of hesitation in the air. I definitely don't get the sense that they're *excited* to see me—no matter what they may have said to Fiona. Maybe it's because they're casting the lead in a big budget studio movie, so they're used to dealing with bigger stars, and better at hiding their true feelings.

"We realize this is last minute for you," one of the women says, and of course now I can't remember her name or what she said her particular job is, but I'm definitely getting a "casting director" vibe off her. "But as I'm sure your agent told you, we're coming up against a firm deadline. Have you read the script?"

"Just now, but only once," I say. "And I know everyone always says they love it, but I really did love it." She smiles, and I add, "Everyone always says that too, don't they? Well, I guess you'll have to take my word for it, although I'm happy to take a lie-detector test."

Everyone snickers, and that helps me relax a little. There are two kinds of acting you do at an audition. There's the acting you do for the actual role itself, reading from the script or whatever. And then there's also the acting you do when you're trying to suck up to the casting director and the producers. You're trying to communicate that you're personable and professional, not some diva who'll embarrass them by showing up late for his call-time or returning from his trailer looped up on Xanax. As any actor will tell you, both kinds of audition acting are equally important.

The casting director hands me an actual printed script, bound with copper brads, and says, "Why don't we start with the cocktail party scene on page twenty-two? Just the monologue?"

"Sure thing," I say, taking the script, then paging my way to the scene she's talking about. At the same time, I try to center myself. This is the first actual acting I've done since *Hammered* went into hiatus—since before Russel's wedding—and for a moment I'm not sure I can. How does a person pretend to be someone else anyway? It's obviously not real, so how do you make it convincing?

I start to read. Zach is seeing Maggie for the first time since the earthquake, and he's talking about the hospital food. But the subtext is all about their previous encounter.

And then I'm there: I *am* this character. I've only read the script once, but I know this character at this point in the script—that he knows how badly he screwed up, and how desperately he wants to reconnect with Maggie.

I'm in the moment, and it goes on and on.

When I finally stop, I feel a little bit like a swimmer coming up for air, breaking the surface of the water. It's that abrupt.

The whole room is silent. They know I was good. They know that I understand this character, and now they're seeing him in a way they didn't see him before. The words on the page have been turned into a real person.

Finally, the casting director says, "Thank you so much, Otto. That was really nice."

"Thanks," I say.

The three people at that table glance around at each other, and I'm a little confused by this subtext. I know to the core of my being that I was good, and I'm almost certain they know it too. My eyes meet those of the videographer, and he gives me a little nod. Even he knows I was good.

So why are the others still hesitating? Why aren't they asking me to do it again? Or read a different scene? Is it my scars again? But this feels different from that somehow. So maybe it really is the lead-in-a-studio-film thing.

Finally, I say, "Would you like to hear another scene? How about the scene on the steps of the library?"

And everyone immediately perks up. I'm not imagining things: they're liking what I'm doing, and they're impressed that I know exactly which scene would be good after only reading the script one time.

So I read the scene, with the casting director doing the other lines, and I dive perfectly into this moment too. I say the words and I hang there, suspended inside this other human being.

And then I break, and Zach slips away, and I'm back to being me again. I look at the eyes that are staring at me, absorbing their interest. The videographer whistles appreciatively.

Now I know for a fact they all think I was good.

But suddenly the vibe in the room is even weirder than before. Folding chairs squeak. Throats are cleared. It's not quite "Don't call us, we'll call you," but there is something no one is saying. I've done a lot of auditions in my life, and I've never felt anything like this before— the mixed messages.

"Should I do another scene?" I say.

Everyone reacts sort of sheepishly, and also sort of confused by my question. Which makes me pretty sure that something *is* going on. But I still have no idea what.

The three people at the table look down at its surface, shuffling papers. The videographer fiddles with his dials again.

"Okay then," I say. "Do you need anything else? Fiona emailed you my resume and headshot, right?"

I hesitate a second more, to give someone a chance to say something, but no one really does. So I turn to go.

"Otto?" the casting director says, stopping me.

I turn back.

"Just so you know," she says. "It's absolutely not your fault—we know this was all very last minute."

"What isn't my fault?" I say.

"Well, Julian had to leave."

Julian Lockwood? It's true that he isn't in the room, but I hadn't been expecting him to be. I've done a ton of auditions where the director isn't there. First you audition for the casting director, then later you read for the actual director and the rest of the producers. And you *have* to read for the director. No one ever casts anything from audition tapes alone. So I'm still confused by what's going on.

"Okay," I say. "So do you need me to come back tomorrow? I'd be happy to, it's really no—"

"He's not coming back," the casting director says. "He had to leave town. He stayed as long as he could, but he had a commitment tonight, and he really had to go."

Suddenly all the subtext in the room makes sense: these people really do think I'm right for the part, or at least I could be, but it doesn't matter because they're not the ones who get to make the final decision. And the guy who does has already left town, and he isn't coming back.

"So..." I start to say.

"We're really very sorry," the casting director says, even as the others start standing up, one by one, indicating that the audition is over. The cameraman snaps the cover over the lens on the camera, and it echoes loudly in the empty room.

I didn't get the part. I never had a chance at the part, not after being held up in traffic and ending up late to the audition. This was just a courtesy read, but for me, because I'd come all the way in to see them.

I think: No! I'm right for this part, I was in the moment. Worse, I know that the people in front of me also think I'm right for the part—they think I can do it too.

I came so close. And it's the lead role in a great script, produced by a major studio and directed by an Oscar-winning director.

"I'm really sorry, Otto," the casting director says. "But you really were terrific, and I'll definitely keep you in mind for future projects."

This sounds like a nice thing to say, and I'm sure she means it, and it might even be comforting to most other actors. But I know that film projects that I'm actually right for that don't involve me terrorizing teen-agers in their dreams are a lot fewer than this casting director seems to think.

CHAPTER FOUR

I can't bear to go back to my apartment.

It's partly everything that happened in the audition—I really need someone to talk to. But it's also because I've spent the last week all alone in that apartment, and I'm starting to go a little stir-crazy. Then there's the fact that I still haven't forgotten that someone who hates me knows exactly where I live. If I went home now and found more melted candle wax splattered on my door, I'm not sure I could handle it.

My friend Russel Middlebrook lives in Hollywood, which is sort of on the way home, at least if I go a different route. By now, it's been a week since his wedding, so I text him to ask if I can stop by, and he says yeah, sure, he'd love to see me.

He and his husband Kevin live in an apartment building right up the hill from old Hollywood—a few blocks from the Chinese Theatre. It's one of those buildings that's been there forever, simultaneously dumpy and also kind of cool, where you can imagine starlets living back in the 1950s. It smells like bacon grease and history.

When Russel opens the door to his apartment, I'm about to tell him what a great time I had at his wedding.

But before I can speak, he says, "What is it? What's wrong?" Russel has dark red hair and the lightest smattering of freckles on his nose, but right now his brow is wrinkled with concern. He sees something on my face.

I go inside and take a seat. Russel and Kevin aren't rich—Russel's a screenwriter, a really good one, but hasn't sold anything yet, so he makes his living as a barista. Kevin is an editor at IMDb.com. And so their apartment is pretty modest compared to mine: a saggy couch, cluttered shelves. I can't help but notice that it smells lived in, unlike mine. It's nice, musky, a little lemony—like two handsome men.

"Tell me what happened," Russel says, so I go off about *The Tulip Vase*, what a great project it is, and also how perfect it was for me. And then I tell him about the audition, how I was good, and how everyone else thought I was good too, but that the director had to leave town. I also mention how *Hammered* was canceled.

"Oh, man, I'm sorry," Russel says. "Truly! That really, really bites." He thinks for a second, then stands. I start to say something, but he holds up a finger, silencing me.

I follow him into the kitchen, watching. He gets glasses out of the cupboard.

At first I think he's going to pour us whiskeys or something, but no, he assembles the blender, then pulls a bottle of rum out from one of the cupboards, and snatches a bag of frozen fruit out of the freezer, and fills the blender with ice.

A few minutes later, he's whipped us up a couple of frothy, colorful drinks, and somehow they seem perfectly appropriate to the situation. Whiskey would seem like we were giving in. But these drinks, which might as well have little umbrellas in them, have more of an impish, defiant feel. It's like they're saying: Yeah, okay, you won this one, you shitty universe, but this thing ain't over yet.

He hands me my glass and says, "There. Drink!"

I smile for the first time since the audition—maybe even for the first time since I was on that plane a week ago. And then I do drink: fruity and frothy or not, it's strong.

"Now," Russel goes on, leading me back into the front room, "continue, please."

At this, I laugh. It actually feels good. *I* feel good, and I know it's not the alcohol since I only just drank it, so it must be Russel.

He and I met as counselors at a summer camp when we were sixteen years old. We dated all that summer and a little bit after. He was my first love—and also the first person I ever had sex with. But back then, we'd lived in different parts of the country, and I had even less self-esteem than I do now. I'd been certain it was only a matter of time before Russel broke up with me. So I pretended I was interested in this other guy, and I broke up with Russel. I'd known it was a mistake right after I did it, but I felt too stupid to take it back.

We stayed friends after that, and Russel dated a lot—first Kevin, then some other guys, then Kevin again. My own love life had been completely non-existent, and I'd been jealous. I kept expecting my feelings for Russel to go away, but he was my first love, and a really nice guy, so they never truly did. So I backed off, and finally we'd drifted apart. I never have told Russel the truth about any of that.

Two years earlier, Russel had moved to Los Angeles to become a screenwriter. At the same time, I'd been trying to make it as an actor, and we'd reconnected. There had been a couple of moments when we were alone together, and I wondered what Russel thought of me—*if* he still thought of me. I mean in a romantic way. But he was with Kevin by then, and I don't think of Russel that way anymore, so nothing had ever happened. Now the two of us are just good friends.

Sitting with him in his apartment, I down my drink and tell Russel everything that Fiona had said to me before Greg had given me *The Tulip Vase* script—that I've only been famous for a little over four months, and my career is looking increasingly washed up.

"Well, that's just stupid," he says. "Have you considered that maybe the problem is Fiona?"

Fiona represents screenwriters too, and she handled a project of Russel's that didn't turn out very well, so I know he doesn't like her.

"I don't think that's it," I say. "She was really excited about this new script."

Russel is about to say something else when Kevin enters through the front door. He's pretty good-looking, with a great five o'clock shadow. Sometimes he wears contacts, but now he's wearing dark-rimmed glasses, which make him look smart and sexy.

"Otto!" he says, happy to see me, and I'm not sure if I shouldn't be a little insulted that he comes home and finds me, Russel's ex, alone with his husband, and he doesn't seem to have even the slightest hint of jealousy or suspicion. Then again, they have a pretty great relationship.

Russel explains about my day, and Kevin gives me a series of sad looks. I said before I wanted pity, but I don't want it now, especially from Kevin.

But toward the end of the story, Russel turns to me and says, "Wait. Where did he go? The director."

"Huh?" I say.

"Julian Lockwood. Why couldn't you go to him? Wherever he is, take a plane or something. If everyone was as interested as you say, you'd think they'd be at least willing to let you do that."

Could I go to Julian Lockwood? I feel a little embarrassed that I didn't think of this myself.

I call Fiona's office then and there.

"Oh!' Greg says when he realizes it's me. "I was just about to call you. I've been on the phone with Emma from *The Tulip Vase*. And can I just say? They really liked you."

"They did?" Even when you're absolutely certain about something, like I was about that audition, it's still nice to hear you were right.

"Yeah, and they told me about the problem with Julian Lockwood—how he had a last-minute meeting with a cinematographer. I'm so sorry, but I guess we had no way of knowing."

"That's why I'm calling," I say. I ask him about me traveling to see Julian Lockwood, to meet him wherever he went.

Greg thinks for a second, then says, "It's worth a shot to ask! We'll call you right back."

I disconnect the phone, and Russel and Kevin stare at me.

No one says anything for a second.

Then Kevin says, "I bet they'll let you. I mean, why wouldn't they?"

I know he's only trying to be supportive, but this sounds patronizing.

"No matter what happens," Russel says, "I'm really impressed. You were up for a part in a Julian Lockwood movie!" Then he proceeds to go off on his favorite scene in Julian Lockwood's last movie.

My phone rings, and I answer it, interrupting Russel.

"Can you be in San Diego by ten o'clock tomorrow morning?" Greg says.

"San Diego?" I say. "Sure thing. I'll leave tonight and spend the night there."

I hang up the phone, but immediately feel strange. I've spent the whole last week by myself, and the last thing in the world I want is to drive all the way to San Diego alone. Still, I know this is an amazing opportunity.

"You want company?" Russel says suddenly. "On your trip to San Diego?"

"Really?" I say. I can see how he figured out what I'm doing by listening in, but what told him how I feel about it? Could he see it on my face?

Russel turns to Kevin. "Hey, Hubby, do you mind if I—"

"Go with him?" Kevin says. "Sure, I've got this project due, so I'm going to be crazy-busy the next few days anyway."

Russel looks back at me. "What do you say? I don't work tomorrow, so I could totally go."

"You're really serious?" I say.

"Sure! It'll be fun."

I look back and forth between Kevin and Russel, and I see how they're both smiling at me, especially Russel. If he and I take this trip, we'll be spending a lot of time together, even staying overnight, but Kevin doesn't look worried at all. He and Russel really do seem to totally trust each other, and I can't help feeling a little jealous about what a great thing they have, and also still a little pissed off that Kevin doesn't see me as even the slightest threat.

"All right," I say. "Let's do it."

Russel ponders for a second, then adds, "Just so we're clear, you're paying for everything, right?"

I make a reservation at the hotel where Julian Lockwood is staying while Russel throws some clothes into a bag. In any normal city, we'd then drive to my place so I could pack a few things, and we'd head out of town. But we live in Los Angeles, where the monster truck rally that is our traffic is especially insane this time of day. So instead we go get some dinner at a nearby Panda Express, wasting time until rush hour is over. Only then do Russel and I go to my place so I can pack my bag, and we finally hit the freeway south of town.

As we drive, Russel says to me, "So tell me more about this script."

"Oh, it's fantastic," I say, describing the story, then telling him my thoughts about turning the main character into a burn survivor.

When I'm done, he says, "That does sound great. And you're right, casting you really does make the story stronger."

I keep talking about the movie, and how excited I am, and all my ideas for playing the part. We're almost to Oceanside when I realize that I've been monopolizing the whole conversation.

"Sorry," I say, "I guess I've kind of been going on."

"No!" Russel says. "It sounds like a really cool project. I'm excited you're so excited."

"Well, what about you? What are you working on lately?

He tells me about a screenplay he's been working on, about a weekend gay wedding, and then halfway through, aliens attack.

"Ha," I say. "That's great."

"It started out as a joke at my wedding," he says, "and I loved how different it sounded. But now..."

"What? It sounds really fun."

"I think it's too different."

"Too different?"

Russel shakes his head. "It doesn't matter."

"Oh, come on," I say. "I've been talking non-stop since Anaheim. How is it a bad thing that your screenplay is too different? Isn't that what you screenwriters are supposed to do—write us something different?"

Russel scoffs. "You'd think so, wouldn't you? Everyone is always saying that. 'Give us something new!' 'Write something no one has ever seen before!' But no one means it. Not the audience, and especially not anyone in Hollywood."

I look over at him.

"Look, when it comes to the movie studios, I get it," Russel says. "There's too much stuff out there, too much media clutter. People are always going to go to see the new *Harry Potter* movie, unless it's really, *really* bad, and maybe even then. But some crazy new movie? If it's bad, no one's going to go, and that's a hundred million dollars down the hole. So I get what the studios are thinking: play it safe, don't make waves, go with what works, even if that means making mostly sequels and remakes and reboots. I think it's a complete dereliction of their mandate as creators of worthwhile entertainment, but hey, first and foremost, Hollywood is about making money, and it always has been. What makes *me* angry," Russel finishes, "is the audience."

"The audience?" I say.

"They don't *want* anything different!" he says. "It's partly they don't understand that for every *Star Wars* movie that gets made, every new Marvel universe movie, that means there's one less other studio movie made. There's less of a chance of some *future* movie they might love. I get that they want to see more of the movies they already like. In a way, I do too. But it drives me so crazy..."

"What does?" I say, smiling at Russel's rant.

"That everyone is so okay with the same thing over and over again! That people don't ask more of Hollywood. They always accept the same old crap, at least as long as the CGI is good, or if it stars some idiot from *Saturday Night Live* who was never funny in the first place."

"Now you're really tilting at windmills."

"Well, you *asked*. The older I get, the more I think that for most people, movies and TV are like comfort food. They like it *because* it's familiar. It makes sense. They know how to respond, what to feel. Sure, they get tired of trends after a while, but it takes a long, *long* time. That's why we had all that vampire stuff, then all the zombie and dystopian stuff. And superheroes— Lord, don't get me started on superheroes. It's the same thing on TV. I look at some of these shows, and I think, 'Really?' Especially the traditional networks. I mean, how many zillion times do they expect us to...?"

At this, Russel stops and his eyes go wide.

He looks at me, his face flushed. "Oh, Otto, I didn't mean—"

I smile again. "Russel, it's okay. I know *Hammered* is a piece of shit."

"Oh, okay, good," he says, and that does sting a bit, because I didn't expect him to agree with me quite *that* fast.

"Anyway," he goes on, "sometimes I think the only people who want something different are people like us, the people who actually make the movies. Or," he adds bitterly, "*want* to be making them."

I think about all this. "*The Tulip Vase* is something different."

He nods. "It is, isn't it? I mean, that ending is fantastic—really something new. But that's kind of exactly what I'm talking about. It's different, but it's not *too* different. It's not aliens-invading-a-gay-wedding different. The rest of the movie, it follows the rules of its genre. In fact, that's why the ending works. It sets us up for a nice surprise. I think that's the key. I mean, sure, there are movies that are totally different—stuff like *The Lobster*. And *Swiss Army Man* with Daniel Radcliffe. But those are movies that are different for the sake of being different. They're also arthouse movies that no one sees. If we're talking movies for mainstream audiences, you can be different, but you can't be *that* different."

"Tarantino's different," I say. "And he broke through to mainstream audiences."

Russel slumps a little in his seat. "Yeah, that's how they screw with our minds, isn't it? Every now and then, someone comes along that blows everything all to hell. And they get away with it. They find huge success. But how often does that happen? No, seriously, you can kind of count them on one hand. And a lot of the times it's all a big gimmick anyway. Diablo Cody? Great, she can write quirky, self-aware dialogue—let's all bow down and hail her like a god. No, I think I'm onto something here, that there's almost always an absolute limit on how different you can be. You can do one thing different, but not three. You can be somewhat different, but not *completely* different."

I've been listening to Russel all this time, interested, but suddenly I can't help but wonder how this applies to me. Am I too different to ever find lasting main-stream success as an actor? I have what most people say is a pretty good body. And I know what Fiona said about being openly gay—how it gives casting directors one more reason to reject me—so I've taken her advice and stayed in the closet for the time being. So now there really is only one different thing about me, not three.

But what *about* my face? That's unquestionably different. Russel had said one different thing was okay, but nothing *too* different. So he thinks it's also a question of degree, and I have a feeling he's right. Are my scars too different? Am I fooling myself when I think there's a real chance I could ever get to play a character like Zach in *The Tulip Vase*?

And all of this only has to do with me being too different to be a successful actor. What about as a person? About being someone's boyfriend? Am I too different for that too?

"The point is," Russel says, wrapping up his rant, "I think lately I've been over-thinking things. I just need to find a story and tell it. Maybe I don't need to reinvent the wheel."

I laugh a little.

Russel hears and says, "What?"

"I'm remembering when you first moved to Los Angeles," I say, "You didn't know anything. You remember that?"

"Yeah, I was so green," he says. "But that was two years ago. And you helped me. You taught me everything you knew."

"Which, looking back, I see now was almost nothing."

"No, you were great. I remember how much I learned that first time we went to lunch. You know, I still use Gold Bond Ultimate Comfort body powder. I'm wearing it now!"

"And now you're telling me everything *you* know," I say. "All the great things you've learned about writing screenplays."

"Well, it's mostly Vernie's advice." Vernie is Russel's screenwriting mentor. "But you've got a point. I have learned a few things in the last few years. Thanks for pointing that out!"

"Sure thing."

I'm glad I've made Russel feel better, especially after I spent so much time monopolizing the conversation. But the truth is, the things he said about being different made me feel worse.

On the way into San Diego, we stop to fill the gas tank. As we pull into the station, I realize it's self-service, and I'm a little nervous because the smell of gas fumes sometimes reminds me of the accident I had when I was a kid. A couple of times I've even had panic attacks, which makes sense when you think about it, and isn't anything to be embarrassed about. But it *does* embarrass me, which is why I always make a point to get gas by myself. It's also why I've never told anyone about the attacks except my therapist, who wrote me a prescription for beta-blockers. But I realize I left my apartment so fast that afternoon that I forgot to pack them.

I wouldn't care so much if I was alone. If I had a panic attack, I could sit in my car with the windows rolled up until it went away. But I don't want Russel seeing me like that, so I hand him my credit card and say, "Hey, would you mind filling us up while I hit the restroom?"

"Oh, sure," he says, completely clueless about what's going on.

Later, we find the hotel, which is the Courtyard in downtown San Diego. It's a pretty nice place. When we check in at the front desk, I realize I've only made a reservation for one room. But at least it has two beds.

"Is that okay?" I ask Russel.

"Oh, sure," he says.

"Great. I'm rich now, but I'm not *that* rich."

Russel laughs, and I do too, but the truth is it's not only the money that makes me want to share a room with him. Truthfully, I'm a little worried I'd feel like I did the week before when I'd come home to my empty apartment, all sad and alone. Now I'm looking forward to having some company for the night.

It turns out to be a nice room, and after we unpack, I decide to read the script again—I still have the copy from the audition. This time as I read it, I study it, trying to see exactly what the writer is doing in every scene.

As I'm sitting in the chair, Russel makes a call.

"Hey, Hubby!" Russel says.

He's talking to Kevin.

Russel listens, then says, "Yeah, I know, it's only been a few hours, but I miss you too. What are you doing?"

Russel listens some more, then tells Kevin about the trip so far—including the fact that he and I are sharing a room. But Kevin doesn't seem to care. Russel also mentions things about the trip that I hadn't even noticed, like the fact that we passed an *actual* car full of clowns, and that the hotel spa offers a chocolate "therapy" bath. I pretend I'm reading the script, but I can't help listening in.

"Oh, he's good," Russel says, and I know he's talking about me, but I don't look up because that'll make it seem like I am listening in.

A minute later, Russel stands and walks to the far side of the room, around the corner where the bathroom is, like he wants a little privacy. Then he lowers his voice, and the room is pretty big—now I can't make out what he's saying. Even so, I can tell it's something sweet and intimate, maybe even sexy, and it's hard not to feel a little jealous.

The next morning, I'm up way before Russel, who always sleeps late. I have a few hours before my breakfast meeting with Julian Lockwood, so I go to the workout room to burn off some of my nervous energy. Then I take a shower and go over the script again.

Russel is in the shower when I finally leave to meet Julian in the lobby. He and his assistant and I are all going to have some breakfast, then head back to his suite for the audition itself.

I'm in the lobby at ten, but Julian Lockwood isn't, and I immediately have a very bad feeling.

My phone rings, and I can see that it's Fiona's office, but I don't want to answer it because I know it's bad news—that Julian Lockwood won't be meeting me. But I know I can't just let it ring.

"What happened?" I say into the phone.

It's Greg, and he says, "He's really, *really* sorry. He had a family emergency. He had to leave for New Orleans early this morning. He only remembered to call us now from the airport. But he did say he looked at your tapes from the audition, and he really liked them, but they're on a tight deadline. He says he's sorry it didn't work out, but that maybe he'll get to read you for something in the future."

"So that's it?" I say. "It's all over? I don't get to audition at all?"

"Otto, I'm so sorry. I don't know what else to say."

CHAPTER FIVE

When I get back to the room, Russel is standing in the bathroom with a white towel wrapped around his waist, combing his wet hair. He looks surprised to see me, but only for a second.

"What happened?" he says.

I tell him everything.

"Oh, man!" Russel says. "This is the kind of thing that drives me *crazy* about Hollywood. You drive all the way down to San Diego to meet with him, and he treats you like this? It's so typical! People like Julian Lockwood think they're *so* special. Because he won an Oscar, he doesn't have to act like a normal human being?"

"Well," I say, "he did say he had a family emergency."

"I don't care! This is completely unacceptable!"

I like that Russel is so outraged on my behalf. But I'm also suddenly aware how good Russel looks standing there in a towel. It's been a long time since I've seen him shirtless, and he's filled out, and also been working out. And he didn't used to have that hair on his chest—reddish brown, neatly trimmed.

I walk toward the bed and sit. "Well," I say, "I don't know what I can do about it now."

Still in the towel, Russel follows me into the main room and sits in the chair across from me. The hair on his legs is thick too, and even darker than his chest. It's like he's not even aware that this might be distracting.

"Did he say where he's going?" he says.

"New Orleans, I think."

"Well, what if you flew to meet him there tonight? Or tomorrow? Do you think he'd let you audition then? I mean, I hate to enable his rude behavior like that, but at least you'd still be in the running."

I wonder if Julian Lockwood would go for this. I really would do almost anything to get that part in *The Tulip Vase*. I'm also not so keen on going back to my anonymous, empty apartment in Studio City.

I find myself wondering if Russel is wearing anything under his towel—underwear, I mean. The way he's spreading his legs, I'm pretty sure if I glanced down, I could see. And if he *isn't* wearing underwear, what exactly would I see?

But of course I can't look, not with Russel staring right at me.

"I'll call Fiona," I say, pulling out my phone.

Meanwhile, Russel stands and walks to his overnight bag, then pulls out a pair of green briefs. So he *wasn't* wearing anything under that towel. He slips them on at the same time he drops the towel, but he's facing away, so I only catch a brief glimpse of his ass.

"Fiona Lang's office," says the voice in my ear. It's Greg.

Fiona is in a meeting, so I explain my thinking to Greg.

"Let us make some more calls," he tells me. "We'll get right back to you. But I like the way you're thinking!"

By the time I hang up the phone, Russel is fully dressed, which is just as well, because he has a husband, and he and I are only friends now anyway.

He's wearing a short-sleeve blue and red button-down that doesn't go with his complexion, and also cargo shorts. When Russel first moved to Hollywood, he and I had a little talk about the importance of dressing well, of looking successful in the industry, but he hadn't listened. I've never really pressed the point, because he's a screenwriter, and nice clothes don't matter as much for them. But cargo shorts? Really?

"So if they say yes, I'm driving your car home, right?" he says.

"I guess," I say, but at the same time that makes me a little sad. I have a feeling that I wouldn't be any less lonely in a hotel room in New Orleans, and unfashionable dresser or not, it would have been nice to have Russel with me.

When Greg calls me back, he says, "Well, there's good news and bad news."

Once again, I refuse to play this game. "Just tell me," I say. "Do I have the audition?"

"Yes. But there isn't much time. They really want to cast this puppy."

The real bad news comes after I hang up the phone and make some calls to the airlines: Delta Airlines has had some kind of computer crash that screwed up their reservations and grounded all their planes. As a result, all the other flights have booked up for the day—not just from San Diego, but even the ones out of Los Angeles.

"We could drive," Russel says. "I mean, we have your car."

"All the way to New Orleans?" I say.

"Well, maybe you could catch a flight out of Phoenix tomorrow, and I can drive the car home from there. Or we could drive all the way." He starts punching something into his phone. "It's...wow, almost two thousand miles. And, oh dear God, much of that is through Texas. Still, I'm sure we could do that pretty fast, at least if we drive straight through. You know, stopping at motels when we get tired?"

"You'd do all that? What about your job?"

"I'm pretty sure I can juggle my schedule," he says.

I call Greg back, who then makes some more inquiries, then calls me back one more time.

"It's a go!" he says. "I've got you scheduled for a meeting with Julian Lockwood on Thursday at four p.m. And can I just say? I think it's fantastic, what you're doing."

Greg gives me the address, and I hang up the phone. It's Tuesday morning, so we basically have three days of driving to get to New Orleans.

Russel's immediately excited. "*Road trip!*" he says, whooping it up.

"I can't believe you're willing to come with me like this," I say.

"Are you kidding? We're going to have a blast!" But then his eyes dart toward me sort of sheepishly. "Assuming..."

"Yes," I say. "I'm still paying for everything."

* * *

Once we're back in the car and on the road out of San Diego, I sense that Russel is noticeably quiet.

So I ask, "What?"

"Well, you don't have to answer if this is too personal," he says. "But..."

"There's nothing you can ask me that's too personal," I say, but at the same time I think: Is this true? What if he asks me if I was wondering about whether he was wearing underwear under his towel?

Then Russel says, "How much money do you make? I mean, you're rich now, right? That's how you bought this car?"

I laugh. "I wish. For *Hammered*, I made six thousand dollars an episode. And we did a total of fifteen episodes."

"Which means—"

"Ninety thousand dollars total from the show. Plus residuals, but that won't be hardly anything because we were canceled after one season."

"Wow," he says, and I can't tell if he thinks that's a little or a lot.

"But ten percent of that goes to my agent, and taxes are huge. I also have to pay a personal publicist, and a lawyer, and an accountant, and an ad rep, and stylists and consultants. The studio only pays for stuff that has to do with the show itself. If it's a charity event, I pay for everything, and it can be weirdly expensive, especially if it involves a donation. I did one charity event that basically cost me fifteen grand. And you *have* to go to charity events, because the whole point isn't necessarily to support the charity, but to have your picture taken on the red carpet. Which, by the way, the actual red carpet? It's nothing like it is in the movies, where the red carpet leads up to the doorway to the event. They do lay down an actual red carpet— sometimes, anyway—but it's off to one side, and no one else uses it. It's only there for the celebrities to walk down, so people can interview us and photographers can take our picture."

"So you're *not* rich," Russel says.

"Well..." I say, "when you're famous, there are other ways to make money than just your salary."

"I knew it! It's an *Indecent Proposal* kind of thing, isn't it? You all get paid millions of dollars for one night of fantasy sex!"

"No, but I can't say I'd be entirely shocked if that happens. Like, sheiks who are worth billions of dollars? I know there have been offers."

"That is absolutely disgusting!" Russel says. "Unless, of course, we're talking about, like, Alfonso Herrera. Then I'm willing to start saving."

This is the actor who plays the hot priest on the new *Exorcist* TV show, and I can't help but smile.

"So?" Russel says. "Where does the cash really come from? Spill it."

"Well, you want to hear something funny?"

"From you? I wish."

I ignore him. "I did a commercial. For Old Navy?"

"Oh, yeah! I remember."

"And I did another one for this Japanese noodle company. And I made more money from those two things than I made from the entire TV show. Almost three hundred thousand dollars."

"Okay, *now* I'm starting to be impressed," Russel says.

"You can also make money by tweeting things. Somehow I have, like, seven hundred thousand followers. And you can make money by going to certain parties. Once I got paid ten thousand dollars to show up at a thing. There was a whole contract and every- thing, how I had to stay for at least an hour, I had to let people take pictures with me. There are people on *Hammered* who make money by wearing certain brands, or ordering certain drinks in bars."

"No *way*," Russel says.

I nod. "And we also get a lot of free stuff. I mean, a *lot*. I know everyone jokes about Hollywood gift bags, but it's a real thing. They give you everything, all on the off-chance you'll tweet about it, or wear it or use it, and someone will photograph you in it. Although once I got this gift bag with a pair of really expensive silk boxers— I looked it up, they're five hundred dollars each—and I couldn't help but think: The only way this promotion makes any sense is if they think I'm really going to sleep around."

Russel smirks. "And *did* you?"

I'm pretty sure Russel is asking me if I sleep around more now that I'm famous. I guess it's a fair question because it's something I used to wonder about cele- brities before I became one. The truth is, people want to have sex with *anyone* on TV, not just Alfonso Herrera. Most of the rest of the cast of *Hammered* talk like they get laid every weekend—even the guy who plays the old fat dean of the school. I get propositions too, whenever I'm at events, but only ever from women. That's okay though: the whole idea of random sex completely baffles me. Spencer is the only person I've been with in over a year, since before the show debuted. But I'm embarrassed to tell Russel that.

So I say, "Eight hundred thousand dollars."

"Huh?" Russel says.

"That's how much money I've made so far this year. I'm telling you that rather than the details of my sex life."

Russel laughs. "Fair enough."

I really have made that much money, but what I don't say is that I've already spent most of it, on my new apartment, and on the stylists and consultants that the studio and Fiona insisted I hire. I've also splurged too much on new clothes. And I don't tell Russel that all the opportunities I've been talking about only exist when you're "hot," when your star is rising. You don't have to live in Hollywood very long to learn that no one wants you on your way down. And that any money you earn can dry up really fast.

"You wanna hear something *really* funny?" I ask Russel.

"Sure," he says.

I tell him there's a chance I could be named one of *People Magazine*'s 100 Most Beautiful People next year.

As I drive on, I look over at him, shaking my head and rolling my eyes with this whole "Can you believe how crazy that is?" expression on my face.

But Russel isn't laughing now. He looks completely happy for me, not surprised at all. "Oh, my God, that is *fantastic*! I can't believe it, I'm driving to New Orleans with one of the most beautiful people in the world. But I don't think that's funny at all—I think it makes perfect sense. I've always known how incredibly hot you are. But how great that other people are finally seeing it too."

I'm not in love with Russel anymore—he and I are just friends now—but at that particular moment, I really, really like him, maybe more than I ever have before.

Russel and I leave San Diego and drive along Highway 8, through the Cuyamaca Mountains toward the Arizona border. I'm a little on edge about the fact that we've got to drive all that way to get to New Orleans on time, but it's nice to be outside of the city for a change, out on the road. Even when I was *in* the city, so much of my life was inside the television studio. I think it's stupid the way car commercials always talk about stuff like "freedom" and "endless possibility," as if cars have anything to do with that. But at this moment in time, we're soaring along the open freeway with the top to the convertible down, and the wind is blowing through my hair, so it kinda feels like the car commercials make sense.

Still, the land around us is surprisingly dull. It's mostly desert, and not in that, "Wow, there sure is a stark beauty in the desert!" kind of way. This is a dull, brown scrub desert that isn't beautiful in *any* way. But somehow there are still a few houses here and there.

Russel must be thinking the same thing I am, because he says, "There's absolutely no reason why people shouldn't live here, but I can't help thinking to myself, 'Why would anyone *choose* to live in this God-forsaken place?'"

"I know," I say. "What is that about?"

"Part of me wants to go into one of these truck stops and ask the clerk, 'You know you can leave, right?'"

"'Blink three times if you're being held here against your will!'"

Russel snorts, then nods to the desolate landscape around us. "I hate that whole idea that the people who live in places like this are supposedly the *real* Americans. Um, why is that exactly? Because they work with their hands? Because they raise cattle? Why is that so much more important than the stuff people do in the cities— like, you know, curing cancer and inventing the Internet?"

"It just is," I say. "Out here, things are more black and white. Men are men, and women are women. Everyone knows who wears the pants."

"Literally! None of this transgender nonsense."

I laugh. "Right!"

"And that just proves how they're the salt of the earth, huh?"

"What does that mean, anyway? 'The salt of the earth'?"

"It means they drive around peeing out of the back of their pick-up trucks," Russel says.

"What about the women?" I ask.

"I was *talking* about the women!"

At this, Russel and I both crack up.

But then we fall silent, and I feel a little strange— guilty, I guess, for making fun of the people who live here. I try to make a point not to ever make fun of anyone, for obvious reasons.

"But I suppose this is just us being elitist Los Angelenos," Russel says quietly, sort of saying what I'm thinking. "I mean, do you ever look around Los Angeles and see it with the eyes of someone who doesn't live there? The traffic, the smog, the falling-down buildings. I mean, seriously, some young adult novelist should set a book there. To hell with *The Maze Runner*, can they run through downtown Los Angeles?"

"It's true," I say, feeling better about everything.

Right then, a car passes us with a big sign in the back window: *Vote Trump 2016! Make America Great Again!*

And Russel and I both immediately scoff, completely disgusted.

"Oh, God, here we go," he says. "Honestly, how can these people be so stupid to fall for that con man? Do they not care he's a complete idiot?"

"And a total racist," I say. "I mean, 'make America great again'? When was America ever greater than it is now for anyone who isn't a straight white male?"

"Yeah, well, at least there's no way he'll ever win the election."

A little while later, we cross over the California-Arizona border. That's when Russel, who has fair skin, tells me he's worried about the sun, and would I mind putting the top to the convertible back up? The truth is, people who wear hairpieces, even small ones like mine, are never completely relaxed when the wind is blowing through their hair, so I'm happy to comply.

I also realize we sort of need gas again, so I stop on the outskirts of Yuma. I see only self-service stations, not full service ones, and part of me wonders if I shouldn't ask Russel to pump the gas again, because I still really want to avoid a panic attack in front of him. But then I notice how gusty it is outside, how the wind is blowing under the canopy and between the pumps. I climb out of the car, and I'm almost sure I won't be able to smell any gas here—just the dust and pollen of the surrounding desert.

Before the wind stops, I slip in my credit card, then slide the nozzle into the car and let it flow.

But right away, Russel follows me out of the car, stretching his legs.

He sees concern on my face. "You okay?" he asks. The wind is so blustery that he has to talk kind of loud.

"Oh, yeah," I say, shrugging the question off.

I don't know why I've never told him about how I react to gas fumes—why I don't tell him the truth now. But I really don't want to. And for the time being, the wind is still blowing, and I don't smell a thing.

A black pick-up truck with tinted windows pulls up on the other side of the gas pumps. It's one of those trucks with the stupid, oversized tires—more like a kid's toy than the real thing. But I'm happy to have another distraction.

Russel leans in toward me. "Oh man," he says, nodding toward the truck, "how big do you suppose *his* dick is?"

The gas pump chugs, and I smile, but I don't respond. I know what Russel is saying—the driver of the truck probably *is* an idiot—but when I say I don't like to make fun of anyone, I especially mean making fun of people for anything physical. I mean, of course.

"I'm serious!" Russel goes on. He holds his fingers not even an inch apart. "We're talking *this* big."

At this, I laugh, even if it does make me a hypocrite. Russel's still in a cheeky mood from our joshing around in the car, and I'm trying to distract myself from the thought of any gasoline fumes. I see movement on the other side of the gas pumps, but I know they can't hear us, not over the sound of the gusting wind.

"I mean it!" Russel says. "With a truck like that, we have to be talking about a total micro-penis!"

But right then, the wind dies down, exactly when Russel is talking.

The smell of the gasoline is suddenly the least of my concerns. Now I'm more worried if the guy in the truck next to us heard him. We're still out in the open air, and there's a row of gas pumps between us. But Russel was talking pretty loud, and it did get pretty quiet.

I see Russel tense too, standing absolutely still. Our eyes meet, even as the pump keeps glugging. I'm desperate to know if the other driver heard us, but at the same time, I'm not sure I want to know. So I don't step to one side to see if there's anyone there listening.

But nothing happens. No one appears. I smell gasoline at last, but I barely notice—it doesn't conjure up any memories at all—because I'm too focused on whoever might have overheard Russel.

Then the nozzle sticking in my gas tank snaps, meaning the tank is full. Russel and I both jump in surprise.

I know we look like idiots, but I don't care. I jerk the nozzle out, and I'm all set to stick it back in the slot in the front of the pump.

Then the wind starts blowing again. It's not as strong as before, and I was barely even noticing the smell of gas, but I'm still glad the breeze is back.

Russel and I both turn for my car. Russel starts to climb in the passenger side again, and I return to the driver's seat.

Before we can get inside, a guy steps around the pumps, stopping about two feet in front of my car.

He's in his thirties, dressed in denim, and he reminds me of an otter—the actual animal, I mean, not the gay sexual type. He isn't huge, but has a sleek, tight body and a dark close-cropped beard. And his eyes are clear and smart. His car is ridiculous, so I would have expected him to look ridiculous too, but he doesn't.

His jaw is clenched. He might as well be baring fangs. There is no question about whether he heard Russel. But what is he going to do?

Neither Russel nor I is inside the car yet, and I'm not sure what to do. I glance around and see we're the only people around—I don't even see anyone inside the station itself.

The wind blows, still not as strong as before, but it whistles around us, and the man keeps staring. They say that bullies are really cowards, so I stare back, as defiantly as I can. I think of it like a part I'm playing, like I'm someone who's impossible to intimidate, but I can't seem to get into character, into the moment.

Finally, the man says, "Fucking faggots."

Still outside the car, Russel and I freeze. What the guy said is bad, but given what Russel had said about him, I can't say it's entirely unfair.

Now I'm expecting him to saunter confidently away—that's what it *seems* to me like he would do now. But he's as still as Russel and I are, which goes to show how little I understand this scene I'm in, the motivations involved. This man is like the dried guts of an insect spattered on our windshield: he's not going anywhere without a fight.

Russel and I exchange a glance across the roof of the car, then we're the ones who move, both of us climbing inside—to hell with our dignity.

He watches us, sees that we're running scared. Once inside the car, I think about whether I should lock the door, but I don't know if that would make things better or worse. I also smell gasoline again, probably on my hand, but that's still the least of my worries.

A smile creeps across the man's face.

Only now do I realize that I've forgotten to get my receipt from the gas tank. I look over, and I see it's ready now, flapping in the wind.

Still the man smiles. The wind is blowing really strong again, and his clothes flutter, but the man doesn't budge. There's no way he can identify me from that receipt, is there?

"Go," Russel says to me. "Just go."

So I put the car in reverse, backing away from the guy in denim. Then I drive away, and I tell myself I'm not going to look back to see if he's still standing there under the canopy. But then I do anyway, and of course he's there, eyes locked on us, watching us leave.

Back on the freeway, I'm still shaken by the encounter at the pumps.

"That was all my fault," Russel says. "Otto, I'm really sorry!"

"No," I say. "It's okay. He was a jerk. I guess it's karma because of all the mean things we were saying earlier about the people who live here. Maybe we deserved it."

"Karma, huh?" Russel says. "God, I hope not."

I glance over at him. "What?"

"Well, if it really is karma, this would be like in one of those road trip movies. You know, like *The Hitcher* or *Jeepers Creepers*? It seems like this is how it always starts. They're driving along, and they do something dumb, something they barely even think about. What did they do in *Joy Ride*? They play a prank on that truck driver named Rusty Nail? Then he spends the rest of the movie hunting them down, determined to get revenge."

I feel myself flush. I glance over at Russel.

"Otto!" he says quickly. "I wasn't serious. I'm sorry, I shouldn't have made that joke. That was just really stressful back there, so I was trying to lighten the mood. But it was stupid, and I shouldn't have said it."

"It's okay," I say.

"No, really, it was dumb."

"It's fine. It wasn't any big deal. It's all over and done now anyway."

But that's when I look behind us one more time, and I see the black truck with massive wheels rising behind us like a storm on the horizon.

CHAPTER SIX

The black pick-up truck zooms toward us like a tidal wave.

"Russel!" I say, my eyes still locked on the rearview mirror.

He senses the warning in my voice and jerks around.

"Are you fucking kidding me?" he says.

"Maybe it's nothing," I say. "A coincidence. Maybe he left the gas station, and he just happens to be going the same direction as us."

But even as I say this, I see how fast the truck is going, how it's bearing down on us, and I know this is no coincidence. I can hear its engine revving from a hundred yards away.

I grip the steering wheel. I don't smell anything now, not the gasoline on my hand, not desert dust, but maybe I do catch a hint of my own sweaty fear.

In seconds, the truck is right behind us, tailgating with a vengeance. The front of the truck is only inches from my back fender. The truck is already so much bigger than my little Mini-Cooper, and the jacked-up wheels make it seem ever larger. The driver may have seemed like an otter before—something potentially dangerous, but sleek and compact—but now his truck feels like a massive shark about to swallow us whole.

"What the *fuck*?" Russel says, squirming in his seat.

I speed up, but of course the truck speeds up too. I can see this was a stupid idea—that no matter how fast I go, the driver of the truck will always go faster. But if I slow down, will he do that too? Or will he plow right into my fender?

We're going fast now, a lot faster that I want, and I realize I've already fallen into his trap, that this was exactly what he wanted. I look around the freeway, and the only other cars are far ahead or way behind us, which somehow figures. Other than that, there's only desert on all side—no exits, no houses.

"I don't know what to do," I say.

"Don't do anything," Russel says. "He's trying to intimidate us."

And it's working, I think. But I don't dare slow down. Outside the car, hot desert air rushes by, whistling in the window seams.

"Fuck this asshole," Russel says. "I'm calling nine-one-one."

I clench the steering wheel tighter still, but my palms are so sweaty now that I can't get a good grip.

Behind me, the truck brakes and falls back a little, but I know it can't be because he's given up.

Sure enough, the truck swerves into the opposite lane, then zooms up next to us on the left, holding steady. It looks even bigger next to me than it did behind. I glance over, and I have to look up to see the tinted windows, but they're dark and I can't see inside. The truck's giant wheels spin next to me, round and round, like they're trying to hypnotize me.

I brake, slowing down, but the truck brakes too, staying absolutely even.

I don't even bother speeding up.

"There's no signal," Russel says, meaning his phone.

"What if I just—?" I start to say.

The truck cuts toward me, and I flinch, expecting a crunch in the metal of my car that never comes. I'm going too fast to swerve hard, not unless I want to lose control of the car, but I do angle the car off to one side.

Of course he follows me, pushing right into my lane. I'm halfway onto the shoulder now, loose gravel clattering under the car.

I have no idea what to do. Do I pull all the way over and stop in the weeds? But if I did that, who's to say he wouldn't stop along with us? So do I swerve toward *him*—try to intimidate him back? Honk for help?

I keep clenching the steering wheel, feeling completely helpless. Russel must be feeling helpless too, because he doesn't say anything, just sits there twisting in his seat and clenching the armrest.

The truck hits the gas, engine revving, pulling ahead, then swerves back directly in front of me.

I slow down, but the truck slows down too. We're barely going fifty miles an hour now, but even that seems pretty fast.

His bumper is right in my face, almost like it's his ass, like he's mooning me. There's a sticker that reads, *If Babies Had Guns, They Wouldn't Be Aborted!*

I glance around, but there are still no other cars around, and I've never felt so helpless and alone, even with Russel sitting next to me.

"It's okay," he says. "Keep driving. He's trying to scare us. But everything's going to be all right."

I nod and think to myself that Russel's timing is pretty good. This is exactly what I need to hear.

Up in front of me, I catch movement on the right side of the truck. He must have lowered the window on the passenger side, and now something is sticking out—a shoulder, thick and muscled.

The driver isn't alone. There's someone with him, someone sitting in the passenger seat.

I see his hand now, and he's holding something—a can of pop.

He throws it, and the can comes flying back toward us, still full, spraying brown liquid as it spins.

I swerve again, as much as I reasonably can, and the can flies by my car, missing us, but a big blotch of cola splashes against my windshield. At least I don't lose control of the car.

"Great!" Russel says. "That was *great driving*, Otto." And I do feel a little burst of pride, even if I'm still terrified out of my mind.

But I honk, laying on the horn full-stop. It's loud and shrill, and probably won't make any difference at all, but I'm tired of feeling helpless, of not reacting in any way.

I'm still honking when the arm appears again, holding something else—something long and narrow, shiny in the sunlight, maybe metal.

A wrench! If that hit my car, it could do real damage. And even if that misses, what else might they have to throw? A crow-bar? A tool box?

If Babies Had Guns, They Wouldn't Be Aborted!

I see that bumper sticker and think: Maybe they even have a gun.

An exit sign looms.

But the whole area around us is only empty desert. Which means that if they realize I'm exiting, and if they exit along with me, we could be alone with these assholes on some deserted stretch of road.

I have no idea what I should do. In front of us, the jacked-up wheels on the truck churn like millstones in a windmill, and Russel and I are about to be crushed.

"There's an exit," Russel says, but somehow he says it more like a question, like he isn't sure that exiting is the right thing to do either.

The man in the passenger seat leans farther out of the window this time. From where I am, I still can't see his face, just more of his muscled arm, but I can tell he's trying to get a better aim.

The exit approaches fast.

The truck rushes by the entrance. We zoom by too.

The arm throws the wrench.

It spins even as it flies directly for my windshield, like some kind of evil boomerang.

I jerk right, tires squealing, into the gravel-covered meridian that now separates the highway from the exit.

The wrench whirls by, missing us by inches, disappearing into the wind.

But I'm going so fast that when I jam on the brakes, the vehicle quakes and swerves. Am I going to lose control this time? No, I'm still clenching the steering wheel tight, ignoring my sweaty palms, and I keep the car on track.

I slip the car into that exit ramp like a practiced nurse slipping a needle into someone's vein.

The ramp angles down, curving into a little valley below the level of the freeway. In other words, it's even worse than I thought because we won't be visible to the passing cars.

For the time being, I can still see the freeway, so I glance over.

The truck with the jacked-up wheels slams on its brakes, swerving over to the side of the road. All they need to do is back up a hundred feet or so, then they can follow us down the exit ramp too—and we'll be alone with them.

Suddenly this seems like a really stupid plan.

I keep gliding down the ramp, and the black truck winks out of sight.

At the bottom of the ramp, I have a choice. Do I go straight, onto the next ramp back up onto the freeway? Or do I go left, under the freeway, or right, off into the boondocks?

For the time being, I decide to stay exactly where I am, unmoving at the stop sign.

I look behind me in the rearview mirror, but the black truck doesn't appear. Russel clenches his cell-phone and looks behind us too. He reminds me of a deflated inner-tube. I can tell we're both holding our breath.

The truck still doesn't appear. And I finally let myself exhale.

Then it's there, big and black, barreling toward us down the exit ramp.

Russel and I both tense.

But wait, it's a pick-up truck, yes, but not the one with the big wheels. It's a different vehicle entirely.

I pull my car off to one side of the ramp, letting the truck pass, and we wait a little longer, and another car appears, but the truck with the big wheels never does. The air conditioner blasts out cold air, and my whole body is drenched with sweat now, and I shiver.

I consider saying to Russel, "What do you think? Are we okay?" But I don't want to jinx us, so I don't say anything, just sit there shivering, and Russel doesn't say anything either.

Finally, still without saying a word, I pull back onto the road, then cross the street onto the other ramp back onto the freeway.

I take it slowly, scanning the road ahead and behind, on the lookout for any sign of the truck. But I don't see them anywhere.

Finally, I'm back on the main freeway, and somehow there are cars all around us now—there's even a state patrol officer. We drive onward for about five minutes, both of us basking in the safety of the other cars. Is this what little fish in schools feel like when they're surrounded by bigger fish in the middle of the open sea?

"Okay," Russel says at last, "that really *was* my fault. I was the idiot who brought up the stuff about how this was so much like a road trip movie."

I don't laugh. Even now, I'm still clenching the steering wheel, still shivering in the cold of the air conditioner.

"Otto?" Russel says, looking over at me with concern. "Are you okay?"

I don't answer. I'm not okay. I'm scared. That whole encounter was incredibly creepy from start to finish, and it's left me really shaken. And how do we know it's really over? The guys in that truck are still out there, on the same road we're on. Somehow it feels like we're destined to run into them again.

But my feelings are about more than what just happened. They're about the way people have been harassing me online for months now, and also the fact that someone found out where I live and came to my apartment, and spattered wax on my door and slid that picture underneath it. Maybe the two things aren't really related—maybe being harassed like that isn't the same thing as being chased by that truck, especially given that Russel had said what he'd said about them. But no matter what Russel said, we didn't deserve to be chased, and we didn't deserve to have our lives put in danger. The whole thing is reminding me again how much hate there is in the world, and now it feels more real than it ever has—even more real than it did that night I found the candle wax. Suddenly it feels like the hate is all around me, like it's maybe even stalking me.

Russel puts his hand on my arm, which is nice, because people don't touch me very often. "It's okay," he says. "Everything is fine now. We're going to be okay. Life isn't anything like it is in the movies."

I nod and smile a little. But the truth is, I'm still unsettled because I know that Russel is wrong—that bad things don't just happen in the movies, that sometimes they happen in real life too.

We don't see the truck with the jacked-up wheels again, and we stop at the next rest stop, so I can finally catch my breath. I see that the cola is drying on my car, so I go into the bathroom to get some wet paper towels to wash it off.

When I return to the car, I find that Russel has almost bought out the vending machine—red vines and M&Ms and Doritos and Reese's Peanut Butter Cups.

"I got us the crappiest stuff I could get," he says.

This makes me smile a little.

After I clean the car, we get back on the road, and Russel plays some *Hamilton* from his phone, and that makes it almost impossible to stay in a bad mood.

But when we pass a truck stop, Russel says, "Hey, look, it's a hitchhiker."

I glance over to see someone on the side of the road, thumb raised. She's big and tall, heavier than I expect a female hitchhiker to be, and older too, with short reddish hair that blows in the breeze of the passing cars.

"We should pick her up," he says, but we've already passed her by, so I can tell he's not really serious.

"Yeah, right," I say.

"No, seriously, it's another road trip movie cliché," he goes on. "You know how they always pick up a hitchhiker along the way? And she—it seems like it's always a she, probably because the main characters of most movies are men. Anyway, *she* has some interesting story about how she's running away from an abusive husband or something. And they get to know her, and then at some point, she offers this perfect advice. And then there's a scene where they go their separate ways, and one of them says, 'Gosh, I hope we get where we're going,' and she says, 'Oh, I know you will.' You know, something like that?"

Scowling, I look over at Russel. After that disaster with the truck, he's really going to bring up another road trip movie trope?

"Too soon?" Russel says.

"Too soon," I say.

* * *

At the next rest stop, I check on flights out of Phoenix and Tucson, but they're still booked up, at least until the following day, so we drive on through. I figure I can try again at San Antonio.

By the time we stop for the night, I've finally calmed back down about the black truck with the jacked-up wheels. I've promised Russel that I'd pay for this whole trip, and I want to get us a nice hotel and a really great dinner to show I'm not annoyed with him for what he said that made the driver so mad. But when we look for a place to stay, we're on a stretch of Arizona highway where there *aren't* any nice hotels. So I pick the best-looking motel of the lot. I also think about getting us each our own room, since we've basically spent the whole day together, but I worry Russel could see that as a sign I'm still miffed, so I end up getting us a double again.

On our way to eat at the diner across the street, I spot the female hitchhiker we saw earlier. Someone must have given her a ride and dropped her off nearby. If I point her out, Russel will definitely know I'm not annoyed with him. On the other hand, he'll probably also think it's some kind of sign from the road trip gods, and that we absolutely have to introduce ourselves. So I end up not saying anything.

Once inside the diner, we sit down at our table, and I pick up my spoon and I immediately lean in to Russel and say, "The spoon is *literally* greasy. But I'm not going to tell the staff, because I sure don't want to get driven off the road by another truck—this one driven by an angry waitress."

Russel immediately busts up. "Or an angry cook!"

After that, this becomes a running joke between us. When the food comes, it's terrible, but we tell each other how great it is, how every bite is like delicious ambrosia from the gods, and we pretend like we're making sure that the cook and the wait-staff see us savoring every bite, so there's no chance anyone will get angry and harass us after we leave.

But then the apple pie comes for desert, and it really *is* weirdly fantastic—like, the best apple pie, and maybe even the best *pie*, I've ever had in my life. And the irony of that makes Russel and me laugh even harder than before.

On our way back to the motel, the hitchhiker is long gone, but I see a crow along the side of the road, scrabbling for something in the weeds.

"Oh," I say. "It's Rainbow Crow."

This is a reference to back when Russel and I were counselors at that summer camp as teenagers. He told our campers this great Native American legend about how crows came to be black—how their feathers used to be all the colors of the rainbow but they sacrificed them to help other people, and now you can only see their rainbow colors if you look really hard.

Russel looks surprised, but pleased. "You remember that?"

"Of course I remember it," I say. "I think of it every time I see a crow. And it was obvious way back then that you were a great storyteller."

Even in the dark, I can see Russel blush.

And I know that we are totally good at last—maybe even better than before.

Back at the motel room, Russel calls Kevin again, but then he goes outside to talk. I can hear his voice through the window and the curtains, but I can't quite make out the words.

I feel like I should study *The Tulip Vase* script, so I open my bag and look for it. That's when I realize that I barely have any extra clothing, since I wasn't expecting to be away from home so long. I have my Etro printed polo and my Versace pleated slim shorts, which I'd worn today, and an Armani button-down with my Paul Smith trousers. I have a few pairs of socks and underwear, and a wife-beater tank top, but at some point, Russel and I are going to need to find a washing machine.

"Yeah, it's kind of sad, actually," Russel says to Kevin, outside.

Maybe Russel shifted or something because now I *can* make out his words. I can't help but think, Is he talking about me? Am *I* what he thinks is sad?

I take a step closer to the window, and I regret it as soon as I do. I know I shouldn't be eavesdropping. But even so, I don't move back to where I was before.

"Well, why can't he just come out and say it?" Russel goes on. "Why all this passive-aggressive bullshit?"

Now I'm *certain* that Russel's talking about me, about how I reacted to what he said to the truck driver. I feel terrible.

"Yeah, I guess you're right," Russel says, his voice through the window. "I've never understood that about straight guys, how they're so completely clueless about subtext."

So Russel *isn't* talking about me. I feel like an idiot for thinking he was. Why do I assume that everything always has to be about me?

Russel keeps talking to Kevin, about someone they both know, and Russel's voice sounds different than how it does with me. It's not that he's more loving. On the contrary, he actually sounds a little more blunt, a little harsher. Russel is probably a bit nicer talking to me. But I like the way Russel sounds, because he sounds more genuine. Unguarded. This is the real Russel, honest and true, what he really thinks. He's not pretending to be someone he's not because he feels sorry for me.

"Well," Russel says, "you know him better than me. But if I were you, I'd tell him to take a flying leap."

Russel's voice is different, but it's somehow familiar too. It's like hearing a song you instantly like, but then you remember you've heard it before, that you already know it.

That's when I realize: This is the way Russel used to talk to me, back when we were a couple. It was a long time ago, and we'd both been different people, but maybe we weren't that different, because his voice sounds so familiar now. I can't help but feel a little jealous. I'm trying to think of the last time anyone has talked to me like that, so honestly. When was the last time *I* talked to someone like that? Has there been anyone since Russel?

Suddenly Russel's voice lowers. He's not whispering exactly, but now I can't make out his words. It's funny how jarring it seems—how it can't help but call attention to itself. Is Russel talking about me now—telling Kevin something I said or did today? Why else would he have lowered his voice? Or maybe they're just sweet-talking each other before bed, or even having phone-sex.

Should I move closer—walk right to the window? I'm pretty sure his voice isn't so quiet that I couldn't hear if I was right up against the glass.

I start to take a step, but then think: What the hell am I doing? Russel has been an incredibly good friend to me. Do I really want to know what he's saying in confidence to his husband about me? He's done me a big favor by going on this road trip with me in the first place, taking all this time out of his life. Do I really want to repay him for that by violating his trust?

I go into the bathroom to take a shower, doing my best to drown out all sound of Russel's voice.

Later, Russel takes a shower too, and I lie in bed reading the script for *The Tulip Vase*. The night before, in San Diego, I'd been so nervous about my audition with Julian Lockwood that I hadn't really thought that I was sharing a hotel room with my ex-boyfriend. But now I can't stop thinking about Russel and me, how we're about to spend the night alone together. Right now he's barely five feet from me, in the shower, completely naked.

It's true that Russel isn't "handsome," at least not like most of the cast members on *Hammered*. They all play typical, guy-next-door-type guys on TV, but they're not really typical at all. For one thing, they all won the genetic lottery, with perfect bodies and flawless skin. They also put all this time and effort into looking like they do—hours in the gym, five hundred dollar haircuts, moisturizers and treatments on their faces.

Russel isn't like that. He's real. And that makes him a hundred times more appealing than the guys on *Hammered*. Suddenly I'm feeling guilty that I was being so judge-y about his clothes before. The fact that he doesn't care about stuff like that is part of the reason why he's so great.

I remember back to when Russel and I were to-gether, when we used to have sex. We were only sixteen years old, and it was all very innocent. The first time, I'd been a virgin, and Russel had only been with one other guy.

I'd been so scared about what Russel would think about my scars, the ones on my body. I hadn't taken my shirt off in front of anyone other than my doctor since I'd been about nine years old. Not even my parents. Russel had been great that first time. He'd acted like I didn't even have scars, like they didn't exist. I don't know how he knew it, but it was exactly what I needed. At the same time, he told me how sexy he thought I was.

But as the summer went on, he stopped pretending that the scars didn't exist. He would touch them, and once after sex, he asked me about them—not only how I got them, but what they felt like. Sometimes during sex, he'd even kissed them, and licked and bitten them, which had made me really self-conscious at first, but had then become incredibly erotic. It was like he was having sex with *me*, appreciating *my* body. He'd said I was beautiful, scars and all, and it was the first time anyone other than my mother had said anything like it. And it wasn't until he'd said it that I realized how much I'd needed someone to say it out loud. I'd never have to wonder again: Could someone accept me for who I am? After Russel, most of my boyfriends were pretty good at ignoring my scars, at pretending they weren't really there. But since then, no one had ever done what Russel had done, and made me feel the way he'd made me feel. Which is probably why none of those other relationships had lasted.

The shower turns off, and Russel steps out of the bathroom, and I realize I haven't read a word in the script in who knows how long—that I've been thinking about Russel the whole time. I have a hard-on, but I'm pretty sure Russel can't see, and *won't* see, not unless I have to get up out of bed for some reason.

Russel stands at the sink by the bathroom, combing his wet hair, then brushing his teeth. I'm pretty sure he isn't noticing me, so I peek over at him. He's got a towel wrapped around his waist again, but the towels in this motel are a lot smaller than the ones at that expensive hotel in San Diego, so they cover a lot less. They're thinner too, so things leave more of an outline. Is he not wearing underwear again?

Finally, he takes off the towel, putting it on the rack on the wall, and I see he *is* wearing underwear—his green briefs. I try not to look, but I do take a quick glance at his bulge, which somehow seems bigger than when we were teenagers. But that was so long ago, so many years, that I can barely remember what he'd looked like even back then. And we'd been together at an overnight summer camp, so it's not like we'd been able to have sex in well-lit areas anyway. Mostly, we'd snuck away at night, to swim naked in the lake and to have sex on the beach and other hidden places.

Russel moves toward the bed, and I feel like an idiot leering at him, and I look back at the script. But I can smell him, freshly-showered, even over the cloying scent of motel disinfectant. Russel smells different from the smell of him and Kevin together, back in their apartment—still lemony, masculine, but sweeter. I can also smell that he's put on Gold Bond again, and it's all kind of driving me crazy.

Russel pulls back the bedspread, then leaps onto the bed like a little boy, bouncing around, still in his underwear. Since he's making such a big show of it, I feel like I can watch him more openly now, and I do, even though I make a point not to look directly at his bulge. Still, there's always his abs, biceps, calves, and hairy chest. I smile watching him, because I can't imagine any of the hip, oh-so-cool cast members from *Hammered* doing anything so silly and innocent.

Finally, he falls backward, still on top of the covers, still in his underwear. He scoffs at something.

"What?" I say.

"Nothing," he says.

"Come on."

"Well, Gunnar bought Kevin and me a new bed for our wedding. We've been so happy that we'll never have to sleep on a crappy futon again. For the first time since I moved away from my parents, I've been sleeping in an 'adult' bed. But I knew it couldn't last." He slaps the mattress. "And this is one seriously crappy bed. I mean, it's like the Platonic form of a crappy bed!"

I laugh, even though I'm not quite sure I get the joke.

"Who knew I'd be back sleeping in a crappy bed again so soon?" he says. "It just goes to show how you can never predict what's going to happen next. Life will always surprise you." He thinks about it, then shrugs. "Oh, well, it's only a couple of days."

And even now he isn't getting under the covers, and I'm still trying to avoid looking at the bulge in his briefs, but I'm also wondering if he's teasing me. But then I realize that no, that's not it at all, that he doesn't think of me that way anymore, that from his point of view we're just good friends. He's still thinking about Kevin, the guy he was sweet-talking on the phone a few minutes before.

And that's okay, because it's not like I'd ever act on my attraction to Russel or anything. He's with Kevin now—I was at their wedding a little over a week ago—and I wouldn't ever do anything to get between them. I'm not thrilled that Russel doesn't see me in a sexual way, that he obviously thinks of me only as a friend now. But it's not like how it is with other people, how no one ever sees me in a sexual way, because I know that Russel once *did* think of me that way, back when we were boyfriends at summer camp, and it had been really real.

As I lay there in the bed next to him, I can't help but realize something that I've never quite understood before—something I know I can never tell him.

I'm still a little bit in love with Russel Middlebrook.

CHAPTER SEVEN

The next morning, I'm up before Russel, and I shower, then go out to get us something for breakfast.

On the way back to the motel, I spot the hitchhiker from the day before coming out of one of the other rooms into the parking lot. I feel guilty that I didn't point her out to Russel the night before, but I'm not sure why.

She's carrying an overnight bag, and as she steps out into the parking lot, our paths sort of cross, and I see her closely for the first time. She's definitely big—not pear-shaped, but apple shaped, with at least as much of her weight above her hips than below. She's also tall—probably almost six feet. I wonder about her age. Late thirties? Early forties? With her reddish hair and bulky bosom, she reminds me of the Queen of Hearts, like on a playing card. She even has sort of a regal bearing, an air of authority.

"Oh, hey!" she says. "You're that guy on TV."

"Yeah," I say.

"Really? It's really you? I can't believe it." Her face breaks into a huge smile, and somehow this seems strange for a hitchhiker. Shouldn't she be more guarded, more hard-bitten? Her clothes aren't torn or dirty either. Anyway, there's something about her I immediately like. She's regal, but approachable.

"It's really me," I say, cool and confident.

I'm expecting her to ask for a selfie, and then I can say, "Sure thing." But she doesn't, and that makes me even more curious about her. Maybe she's too poor to have a cellphone.

"Well, good for you," she says.

Most people are friendly to my face now that I'm famous, but I still appreciate the fact that she isn't staring at me because of my scars. So I hold up the sack I'm carrying and say, "You want an Egg McMuffin? I think I got too much."

"Really? Well, why not? Thanks a lot."

I give her one, and she takes a seat on one of the white plastic lawn chairs outside the motel room doors. I'm in a hurry to wake Russel up and get us back on the road so we can get to New Orleans, but I figure it's kind of rude to walk away, so I linger. Besides, I'm definitely curious about how someone like her ended up hitchhiking.

"So, I'm Mo," she says, talking with her mouth full. She nods to the Egg McMuffin. "And thanks again for this."

"Sure. And I'm Otto," I say, in case she recognizes me but doesn't remember my name. "I think we saw you hitchhiking yesterday."

As she eats, she nods. But she doesn't give me any answers about why someone like her is hitchhiking.

Instead, she asks me, "Who's 'we'?"

"Oh. My friend and me."

"Boyfriend?" But she immediately catches herself. "Sorry, that's none of my business."

But now I'm even more intrigued by her. People never think a guy with scars on his face could possibly be gay, so why does she?

"He's not my boyfriend," I say. "But he used to be."

As soon as I say this, I wonder if it's the smartest thing, especially if Fiona wants me to stay closeted in Hollywood. What if Mo posts something online and gets a rumor started? But somehow I'm not worried she will. And anyway, even online, people probably won't think the guy with facial scars could be gay, or have any kind of sex life at all.

"What made you think I was gay?" I say, because I'm really curious.

"Oh, all the hot guys are gay," she says, and I know she's probably being nice because I gave her an Egg McMuffin, but I don't care, because like everyone else, I like it when someone calls me hot. Between this and the *People* magazine thing, I'm on a roll.

"Plus, you're an actor," she goes on. "Isn't everyone in Hollywood gay?"

"Not as many as you'd think. Maybe thirty percent of the guys? Actors, anyway. Not a lot of the women are outright lesbian, but if you throw in the sexually fluid, well, the sky might be the limit."

She laughs. "Yeah, I'm not so big on sexual fluids. Too sticky."

It takes me a second to realize that she's making a joke, but then I laugh too.

"So," I say, "are you hitchhiking again today?"

She nods, but once again she doesn't tell me what I really want to know, which is why she's hitchhiking in the first place.

"East?" I ask, and she nods again.

And before I can stop myself, I find myself saying, "Let me check with my friend, Russel. If you want to, maybe we can give you a ride."

To my surprise, Russel is awake and dressed when I get back to the room.

"Oh!" he says, seeing the bag in my hand. "Breakfast!

While he wolfs it down, I mention how I ran into Mo, who is waiting out in the parking lot.

"The hitchhiker?" he says, excited. "Does she seem okay? Not a serial killer?"

"Well, she admitted to killing three people," I say, "but it sounds like they all deserved it."

Russel laughs. "Did you ask her if she wants a ride with us?"

"I wanted to ask you first."

"Sure! You know, I saw her again last night, but I didn't say anything, because I know how badly you want to get to New Orleans."

Once we're all in the car and on the road again, Russel immediately turns to Mo, wedged in the backseat, and says, "So? What's your story?"

"My story?" Mo says.

"Yeah. Why are you out here hitchhiking?"

I roll my eyes at him, but at the same time, I'm glad he asked the question.

"There's not really a story," Mo says, looking out the window. "I'd never done it, and I was curious."

"Oh, please," Russel says. "There's *always* a story. You're running from something, right? Or *someone*. You're about to get married, but you're not sure you love your fiancé? Except—sorry—you're probably a little old for that. Or...wait. You're going *to* something. A new job opportunity? Some place where you can start over and become someone completely different?"

Mo looks at me in the rearview mirror as if to say, "Is he for real?"

"Russel's a screenwriter," I explain. "And he's convinced that everything that happens to us on this trip is going to be some cliché out of a road trip movie."

"Oh, and I'm the hitchhiker you pick up along the way?" Mo says, excited.

"Exactly," Russel says. "The one with the mysterious secret, who also teaches Otto and me some valuable lesson." He looks momentarily thoughtful. "Okay, you're not running away from an abusive past..."

"Not unless you count my phone contract with Verizon," Mo says.

"Which means," Russel goes on, "you must be going *to* something—or doing something important. The father who abandoned you? No, that's not right. You're an inventor on your way to pitch some revolutionary new product? No, that's not it either."

"Sorry to disappoint you, but I'm just an aimless drifter." Mo squirms, trying to get comfortable. The backseat of a Mini-Cooper really is too small for someone as big as she is.

Russel is still considering Mo's motives. "We've already had our run-in with a psychopath," he says, "so we know you're not that."

"Now *that* sounds like an interesting story," Mo says. "But that makes me have a question of my own." She looks at me. "Why exactly haven't you strangled this guy in his sleep?"

Russel and I both laugh

To Russel, Mo says, "So you're a screenwriter? Written anything I might have seen?"

"That depends," he says. "Have you broken into my apartment, logged onto my computer, and read any of my unproduced screenplays?"

Mo smiles.

"He's really good," I say. "I read a lot of scripts, and it's sort of shocking how they all sort of blend together. But Russel's scripts stand out. They feel like no one could have written them except him. He just hasn't had his big break yet."

"I stand out so much no one will even return my emails," Russel mutters.

"It's only a matter of time."

"And you're an actor," Mo says to me, so I explain what this little road trip of ours is all about, how I'm on my way to audition for Julian Lockwood in New Orleans.

"Julian Lockwood?" she says.

"You know who he is?" Russel says. Now he's the excited one, almost breathless.

"No idea whatsoever."

Russel laughs, and Mo says, "So you guys used to be boyfriends, huh?"

Russel looks at me and smiles. "So you told her that?"

I immediately blush.

But Russel shrugs and says, "That was such a long time ago. The two of us were kids at the time. Otto and I are only good friends now."

And then he touches me on the arm again, loose and casual, but this time it doesn't feel quite as good as it did before.

Before long, we cross the border into Texas. Mo does have a cellphone, and around noon, she looks up from it and says, "What do you say we stop for lunch? My treat. There's a place near here that I've heard is pretty good."

"Sure," I say, and Mo directs us to a barbecue restaurant in one of the towns we're passing through.

While Russel and Mo go inside to get a table, I stay behind in the car for a second, calling to check in with Fiona.

Greg answers and says, excited for me, "Otto! How's it going?"

"We're making really good time," I say. "I should be there by Thursday, easy."

"Excellent."

"Hey, can I talk to Fiona for a second?"

"She's on another line right now," Greg says, "but she is so excited for you. She really thinks this is gonna be the one."

The restaurant is one of those fake cowboy barbecue joints, with steer horns and wagon wheels on the walls, and a chandelier made of antlers decorated with Christmas lights. Except this is Texas, so maybe it isn't fake.

But no matter how tacky it looks, it really does smell amazing: a combination of roasting meat, and woodsmoke, and spices—all of it swirled around by ceiling fans.

As I look around for Russel and Mo, I spot her standing by a decorative parking meter, staring out over the restaurant. I figure she's coming from the restroom, and now she's looking for Russel too.

But no, I immediately spot Russel reading the over-sized laminated menu at one of the tables. Mo has to have seen him too—he's right in front of her. Instead, she's clutching her phone and gazing around the rest-aurant itself. There's an expression on her face I can't quite place, and her shoulders have a bit of a slump. Is she horrified by the tackiness—and the cultural insen-sitivity of the totem pole? It almost seems like she's sad.

I step up next to her. "Pretty kitschy," I say.

She starts in surprise, and I realize I've interrupted something. A memory? Has she been to this restaurant before?

But whatever was on Mo's face is long gone now, and her back is tall and proud. She says, "Yeah, well, this is Texas."

When we sit down at the table, Russel barely looks up from the menu and says, "You can tell a good barbecue restaurant by the sides. I know that's count-erintuitive, but it's true. If they don't pay attention to their sides, you can bet they don't pay attention to their meat either."

Mo smiles and reminds us that she's paying, insisting that we order a lot of everything—including sides. So we get chicken, ribs, pulled pork, and lots of sides: baked beans, coleslaw, onion rings, corn of the cob, and corn bread.

Before I can ask Mo if she's been here before, she looks at Russel and says, "So tell me something about screenwriting that I don't know."

"Really?" he says, perking way up.

"Really," she says.

"Well, there's still a lot about screenwriting that *I* don't know. But lately, I'm all about the twist ending."

"That sounds interesting," Mo says.

"Personally, I'm of the school that says that *every* screenplay needs a twist ending of some kind. If the story ends exactly the way you think it will, what was the point of watching it? And yet so many do." Russel sighs heavily. "No, there needs to be something that happens that's a *surprise*—something that focuses the script and reveals the whole point of the story. I mean, it's not until the ending of *Casablanca* that you realize that it's not a love story at all, but a story about duty and self-sacrifice. Looking back, you can see that it's the perfect ending—that that's where the story was going all along. But you don't realize it until it happens. *That's* good writing. When non-screenwriters talk about screenplays, they always talk about the dialogue because that's what people remember. But the dialogue is actually the *least* important part of a screenplay. Far and away the most important part is the *structure*—the step-by-step building of the plot pieces that all come together at the end. That's what storytelling *is*."

"That all makes sense," Mo says.

Russel hesitates. "You're not interested in this."

"No! I am." And Mo does look interested, completely.

Russel looks at me, and I nod too. I'm always curious to hear about storytelling from the writer's point of view. Or maybe I like listening to Russel talk.

"Well," he says, "an actual 'twist ending' takes it even further than that. It's a story where something happens at the end that completely changes our understanding of everything that came before. It has to be fair, of course—it can't come completely out of left field. And sometimes it's something the main character doesn't even learn, only the audience. Like the ending to *Psycho*, when we learn that Norman Bates is, well, psycho, and his mother doesn't exist except as a voice in his head and as a stuffed body down in the basement. That's when we realize that Norman Bates is an unreliable narrator—that we couldn't trust his perspective. But I like the second kind of twist ending more. That's when it's the main character who discovers the piece of information that changes everything. There's even a Greek word for it: *anagnorisis*. According to Aristotle, this is the moment when the main character finally understands the truth about himself. The classic example is when Oedipus realizes that he's unknowingly fulfilled the Oracle's prophecy, and he really has killed his father and married his mother. But there are a ton of movies that use *anagnorisis*—movies like *The Sixth Sense*, where there's that moment when Bruce Willis finally realizes that he's been dead all along, and he's actually a ghost."

I smile. This is so Russel, quoting Aristotle at a Texas barbecue.

"As an actor, I love those moments," I say.

"Really?" Russel says.

"Are you kidding? Those are the moments actors *live* for. I totally agree with you, by the way, that good writing isn't about the dialogue—the witty one-liners. It's about what's going on *under* the dialogue—what's going on in the story, what it all means. It's always nice to get a laugh, but that's not what makes the audience love you. They love you when you make them really, really want something to happen. And then it *does* happen, but not at all in the way they expect. Write something like that, and you'll have every actor in Hollywood lining up to be in your movie."

"It's not the actors I'm worried about," Russel says, releasing another sigh. "It's the people with money— the ones who actually greenlight things."

"Don't worry," I say. "It's only a matter of time." I turn to Mo and say, "I'm serious, Russel really is a great writer."

But when I see her, I realize that Mo hasn't really been listening to our conversation so much as watching us together, Russel and me. Even now, she's considering us with this little smile on her lips.

And I'm dying to know what she's thinking.

Russel may or may not be right about Aristotle and screenwriting, but he's absolutely right about sides in barbecue restaurants: the baked beans are gummy, the cole slaw is flavorless, and it turns out that the meat isn't very good either. But I don't say anything, because Mo suggested the place, and she's paying too, and we're all having a pretty good time anyway. I already feel like I've known Mo a long time.

Back at the car, Russel offers to let Mo take his place in the front seat, but she turns him down, squeezing into the back again.

We drive a few more hours, then we pass a billboard, and I say, "The world's largest toilet brush? So far we've seen the world's largest coffee mug, a flying saucer you can walk inside, and a dinosaur made out of hubcaps."

"Actually," Russel says, "we haven't *seen* any of those things because you have us on such a tight schedule. We've zipped right by them."

I'm tempted to point out that the whole point of this trip is to get where we're going on time, not stop and see tourist traps. But we are ahead of schedule.

From the backseat, Mo looks up from her phone again and says, "I know something else we can see." That's when I know I'm outgunned, so I agree to go where she directs me.

An hour or so later, we arrive at a place called Saddlesore Junction—a tourist-y recreation of an old frontier town, not too far off the freeway. The buildings are painted in bright colors and marked with words like "saloon" and "bank" and "sheriff" and "hotel," but they're all gift shops and ice cream parlors, as far as I can tell. And at this point, I seriously want to bean whoever came up with the first decorative wagon wheel.

We park and get out to look around. There are a handful of people—parents with screaming little kids and bored teenagers staring at their phones. It's fine as far as tourist attractions go, but I admit I'm curious why Mo wanted us to stop here. The walk-through flying saucer sounded way more interesting.

We check out the closest of the gift shops, which is filled with racks of t-shirts, and beaded Indian jewelry, and a cabinet full of some locally made hot sauce and pickled asparagus, and, weirdly, a big collection of ships-in-bottles. In the middle of the Texas frontier?

A few minutes later, Russel tugs on my shirt from behind.

"You have to see this," he says, wanting to show me something.

He leads me to an area in the back of the gift shop—a little wooden storefront within the store with the words "Curio Museum" written on the glass in the fake, curtained window.

It's darker inside, everything lit by wan light in recessed fixtures, but I can make out the glass displays filled with all kinds of strange things—Indian scalps, and rusted torture devices, and cow embryos suspended in jars full of formaldehyde, that kind of thing. Everything is old and dusty, and the signs are all warped and yellowed with the letters faded.

Inside one of the cases, a bulb flickers. Being here makes me a little nervous for some reason.

Russel takes me by the shoulders and leads me to the one of the display cases.

"Look at this," he says, and I can tell there's something he's not saying.

Inside the case on a cloth-covered pedestal is an old box of dark weathered wood, banded with iron, with a big metal padlock on the front.

A sign on top of the box, a little sandwich board, says, *BOX OF MYSTERY: Do Not Open!*

There's another sign on the pedestal itself, and it reads, "Not long after we opened the Saddlesore Junction Curio Museum, a man came to us with an offer to give us one thousand dollars. In exchange, he made us promise to forever keep this box safe, but to never open it up. He wouldn't tell us what's inside, and we never saw him again, but visitors to the museum have speculated that it may contain any number of dangerous things, from the trapped spirit of an evil Indian shaman, to some imprisoned incarnation of the Devil Himself. All we know is that WE WILL NEVER OPEN THIS BOX!"

I roll my eyes. "Really?"

"What?" Russel says. "You don't believe? You really think a place like this would lie?" He smiles. "Come on. What do you think is inside?"

I scowl, but I shiver a little too. Something in this room smells off—musty. They've done a good job of making this stupid museum creepy. Or maybe it happened by accident, because they never clean up or replace the light bulbs.

"There's nothing inside," I say to Russel. "Come on, let's get out of here."

"I think you're wrong," he says, leaning in for a closer look, staring hard.

"Russel."

"No, really, there's something here. Just watch."

And I can't help myself. With Russel staring so hard, I look to see what he sees. But of course there's still nothing unusual.

All of a sudden, the box itself jumps, like there *is* something inside trying to get out.

I gasp, lurching backward. I immediately feel like an idiot, but it was so completely unexpected.

Russel is already laughing at me—he was primed and ready.

"Isn't that *great?*" he's saying. "What I love about it is that this whole museum looks so cheap, you'd never expect them to rig up something like that. Plus, I love how it takes so long between jerks."

But I'm barely listening to Russel now. I find myself facing another display, one with the caption: *MEET THE FREAKS!* There's a mummified body that's supposedly half baby and half alligator, even though it's obviously a dried monkey torso stitched onto the body of a small alligator. There's a skull, supposedly of a demon but probably plaster, with horns and everything. And there are black-and-white pictures too, of all the usual freaks—conjoined twins, tall people, little people.

I stare at all this, unmoving. I'm not sure if I'm breathing, and also what I'm thinking or feeling.

I have a complicated relationship with the word "freak." Or maybe it's not that complicated, because I hate it. It reminds me that if I'd lived two hundred years earlier with a face like mine, I probably would have been locked away in some asylum—or maybe even on display in an actual freak show, especially if I'd never been able to have any of my reconstructive surgeries. The whole idea of a "freak" is so crazy, because it says that people who look or act in a way people don't like are somehow responsible for the way they are—and also for the way people react to them. That really seems like piling on. It sounds silly, identifying with mummies and skulls, much less obviously fake ones inside a glass case in a roadside attraction. But somehow I do.

Russel sees what I see. A little lightbulb appears over his head.

"Oh, God, Otto, I should have realized..." he says. "I'm so sorry!"

"It's fine," I say, and it really is. The truth is, sometimes I get tired of always freaking out over words like "freak." I'm different. So what? The exhausting part isn't being different—it's thinking so damn much about it. Some Box of Mystery I am, always reacting the same dumb way. So at this moment in time, I'm determined to *not* obsess about it. I'm choosing to move right on.

"It's *not* fine," Russel is saying. "I can't believe I brought you back here. This is so offensive. And I'm such an idiot."

Russel isn't getting the memo. So for his sake, I try a different approach. "You really are," I say.

"Huh?" he says, surprised.

"An idiot. And completely insensitive."

"Really?"

I give him a giant, ridiculous nod. "Really. I'm totally traumatized right now, and seething with resentment. But there might possibly be a way you can make it up to me."

"Name it."

"You can buy me a pressed penny with the words 'Saddlesore Junction' stamped on it."

Russel considers this for a second. Then he holds up a firm finger and says, "*Deal!*"

I'm not upset by that display in the curio museum, but it doesn't exactly make me want to shell out for salt water taffy and souvenir plastic tomahawks in the gift shop. So while Russel is using the bathroom, I go outside for some fresh air. But it's hot and dusty, and I realize how very tired I already am of the desert.

A tumbleweed blows down the street right in front of me, and I'm honestly not sure if it's a real tumbleweed or something that was part of Saddlesore Junction—a display or something. Are there real tumbleweeds in Texas?

I spot an old wagon parked alongside the road toward the edge of town. The covered part of the wagon is gone, but it still has the wooden ribs.

Mo sits in the driver's seat, staring off into the distance. The paved road stops at the end of town, but a gravel road continues on, out into low hills covered with scrub and a few trees.

I head toward her down the boardwalk, thinking to offer to buy her a cotton candy or something since she paid for lunch.

She looks down at her phone.

Closer, I see she's sitting awkwardly, almost slumped in the seat. She doesn't look big and regal now, like the Queen of Hearts. She almost looks defeated.

As I move closer still, I can't help but see that she's looking at pictures on her phone, paging through them one by one. No, I realize: there are only two pictures, and she is toggling back and forth between them.

From behind, I see at least one picture is of a covered wagon—probably the same one she's sitting on now, except the covered part has cloth on it in the photo. But I'm too far away to see any more than that.

I remember when I'd seen her back in the barbecue restaurant, when she'd seemed sort of defeated then too. I'd had a feeling she'd been there before, that she was looking for something. Maybe that's why she also wanted to stop at Saddlesore Junction.

Her shoulders shake. Then I hear the first sob.

Mo is crying.

I don't want to interrupt her, so I back away, but the slats in the boardwalk squeak under my feet, and I'm certain that she'll overhear me and turn to see.

But she doesn't. And when she joins us again at the car a few minutes later, her eyes are dry and bright, her back is tall, and there's no sign that she's been crying at all. As an actor myself, I can say her performance is incredible, completely convincing.

It's yet another Box of Mystery—one I'm not sure if I should try to open or not.

CHAPTER EIGHT

As we approach San Antonio, I realize I could try again to get an airplane ticket. On the other hand, the audition isn't until four the following afternoon. We have another six hundred or so miles to go, but we're still making really good time. Besides, I'm curious about Mo—I want to know more about her—and I don't want to make Russel drive all the way home by himself. So I decide to drive on through, and then onward past Houston too, so we'll have less to drive tomorrow.

Finally, we stop at another roadside motel—it looks better than the one the night before but not by much. In the front office, Mo gets a room for herself, and then it's my turn. I consider asking Russel if he wants a room for himself for the night, but then the clerk looks at Russel and me and says, "A double?"

I glance over at Russel, who's perusing a rack of pamphlets. He looks at me and grins, seemingly fine with the idea of our getting another double, so I nod at the clerk. I tell myself that it's still because of everything that's happened lately, how I don't want to be alone right now. But I know even as I think it that's it's a lie, that I'm starting to feel things for Russel I shouldn't.

In the room, Russel passes by me, and I can smell him again, still lemony-fresh, but a bit muskier than before. His Gold Bond body powder might be failing him a little, but I like it.

He starts digging through his bag, and I know he's looking for his earbuds.

"Gonna call Kevin?" I ask.

"Huh?" he says. "Oh, yeah, but I'll go outside."

"No, I'll go. I need some air."

So I go outside and get a cold Pepsi from the vending machine, then sit on the little white plastic lawn chair outside our room—exactly like the chair at the motel the night before.

I can hear Russel through the window, talking about our day, mentioning Mo, how much he likes her. His voice is somehow clearer than the night before, when I was on the inside listening to him outside. Maybe this hotel is less well-insulated, or the glass is thinner.

"Honestly, I'm a little worried about him," Russel says. "I think he's lonely. He's such a good guy."

This time, I know I'm not imagining things—Russel really *is* talking about me. I also know I shouldn't be listening in, and I'm all set to stand up and take a walk. But somehow I can't quite do it.

"I brought him into this little museum today," Russel goes on. "And it turned out to have this freak show part. I felt so stupid. I can only imagine what he was thinking. Part of me wishes there was something we could do."

Russel listens to Kevin say something, then he laughs. Is he laughing at me? Or is it something else? Did Kevin suggest a threeway? I wonder: What would I do if Russel and Kevin *did* suggest a threeway? I've heard gay couples talk about that, but I've never done anything like it. And of course it would be a terrible idea, and would end up making my feelings for Russel so much worse. But I'd still have a hard time saying no. Not that it matters anyway, since Russel and Kevin clearly don't see me as much of a sexual being.

"Quite a drive, wasn't it?" a voice says, and I jump.

Of course it's Mo. I'm embarrassed that I was so intent on eavesdropping on Russel that I didn't even notice her approaching.

"Yeah, sorry about that," I say quickly. "I guess I want to make sure we get there on time."

Mo has a can from the vending machine too, and she doesn't say anything for a second. She takes a sip from her drink, and now we can both hear Russel's voice inside the motel room, and I know she knows I was eavesdropping on him.

I immediately stand. "Go for a walk?" I say, and Mo nods.

There's not really anywhere to walk to—there's not even a sidewalk along the main road—so we start down the gravel strip along the pavement. There are other motels, and restaurants, but they're not all lined up in a row: they're separated by dark vacant lots filled with dried weeds and twisty trees. It's also late at night, and there isn't much traffic, but we're far from any real city lights, so the sky is wide and black. The stars blaze and twinkle, and it's hard not to feel like they're all around you, like you're lost inside it all, like you're part of an explosion.

I start to laugh.

"What?" Mo says.

"Well, I live in Los Angeles," I say, "and I can't remember the last time I saw the stars like this, so bright. But I'm laughing because we did this episode of *Hammered* where the guys in the dorm spend this night out by a lake. We filmed a little bit of it on location, but almost all of it was done on a soundstage. There's this scene where we all stare up at the stars, but it was done with green screen—the stars were computer generated. We had to pretend we were looking up at the stars, but there wasn't anything there."

"And?"

"And what I was imagining wasn't anything like this!"

Mo chuckles. "Are you one of those actors who has to feel like what you're acting is really happening? What's that called? Method acting?"

"Yeah," I say. "And here's the truth about that: method actors don't really exist. Not like they say anyway, where the actor has to stay in character all day, or anything like that. I mean, maybe Daniel Day-Lewis, but I bet not even him. Maybe it was a real thing in the sixties, but I've worked with a lot of different actors, and everyone has their own process, but no one acts like that really. I mean, yes, most of us want to feel something real, and we all definitely want to *look* like we're feeling something real. But we always understand that it's not real."

"In the end, it's all just pretend?"

"For the most part."

"Sort of like the way you act around Russel?"

I don't say anything, and we keep walking. I know exactly what she's saying—that she knows I have secret feelings for Russel. But I still don't want her saying it out loud.

Our feet crunch in the gravel, a little out of synch. The air smells like dust and dry grass.

"He's a great guy," Mo says. "He's kind of exhausting, but in a good way."

I don't say anything, but that really is the perfect description of Russel.

"I'm not in love with..." But I stop. I know I can't finish the lie. "Am I really that obvious?"

"Not to him. He has no idea."

"Am I a fool?" I say. "I know I can't be with him. But I still want to be around him. It doesn't feel good exactly. But it makes me feel something. And it's better than what I was feeling before, which was alone."

Mo doesn't say anything as we walk on, but I can tell she's thinking hard. I'm really curious to hear what she has to say. At this moment, she seems very maternal, and I'm having the kind of real conversation that my actual mother and I could never have.

"I lied before," she says. "In the car? When Russel asked why I was hitchhiking? I do have a reason."

I listen, very curious.

"I had a son," she says. "He was twenty years old."

I think: Was?

"He died from a drug overdose. In February."

This hits me a little bit like a punch in the gut. "I'm so sorry," I say.

"Thank you," she says. "He left home last summer— we weren't in a good place. I wanted him to go to college, but he wanted to see the world."

And finally I understand, not just why Mo is hitch-hiking in the first place, but why she wanted to stop at that bad barbecue restaurant, and also Saddlesore Junction.

"You're retracing his route," I say.

Against the outline of the exploding stars, I see her nod. "The last few weeks anyway. I'm using Facebook and Foursquare—the police gave me his phone after he died. I don't know everything he saw and did, but I have an idea."

"But why hitchhike? Because he did?"

"Yeah. And I know it's stupid. I mean, I know he didn't stay in motels—he had a tent and I think he camped most nights—and I'm sure as hell not doing that. But somehow it made sense for me to hitchhike, even though I'm probably going to get myself killed."

I smile in the dark. "Something tells me you can handle yourself."

Walking along the road, we come to a drive-in restaurant—old-fashioned, with cool neon and stainless steel counters, and hand-painted lettering on the over-sized menu. It's still open, and I can smell hamburgers cooking on a grill, but there's no one eating now. The teenager at the window reads his phone.

Mo stops and stares in at the restaurant. The glare of the neon makes her face look blue, and she's slumping a little again. She doesn't look like the Queen of Hearts anymore.

"What will you do when you get to the end?" I ask, but I immediately regret it. The end of her trip, wherever it is, is also the place where her son died.

"I'm not sure," Mo says. "Be devastated. Or maybe I'll have some new perspective. Who knows? The truth is, I don't think it's about getting to the end. I think it's about right now, about being around him, being close to him—as close to him as I can be at this point. It's like what you said about you and Russel, how you need to be around him. What I'm doing, it doesn't feel good, but it feels better than what I was feeling before."

"It's not the same thing. Losing your son—it's not the same thing as my having a dumb crush on Russel."

She looks over at me, and I realize we're both bathed in blue.

"Maybe not," she says, "but it's what made me tell you. My friends would think I'm crazy if they knew what I was doing. They think I'm at a grief retreat in Arizona right now. I haven't told anyone—you're the very first. No one has any idea, so if I do get killed somewhere out here, no one will ever know. But I had a feeling you might understand."

"What was his name?" I ask. "What was he like?" I'm tempted to ask if her son was gay, but I don't want to make Mo feel even worse if that's part of the reason why he ran away from home. And it doesn't matter anyway.

"Eric," she says. She thinks for a second, then looks up at the sky. "He was like the stars—so bright, so beautiful, but so far away. Impossible to touch. I don't think he let very many people see his true self, because he was worried about what they'd say. That they might reject him." She looks back down, directly at me. "He was a lot like you."

No, I want to say. If he really was like me, he wasn't hard to touch. He was right in front of you the whole time. But he was worried you wouldn't want to touch *him*. And you wouldn't want him touching you back.

But of course I don't say this.

"I think that's what our argument was all about," she says, "the one we had before he left for the last time. I didn't understand how important it was for him to go. That's probably why he felt like he had to. Looking back, I wonder how clearly I ever saw him. How much my impression of him was of the person I wanted him to be."

"Mo—"

She holds up a hand, stopping me, shaking her head. Then she takes a breath, and straightens, and even bathed in blue neon, suddenly she's back to being the Queen of Hearts—the person she was before she'd told me the truth about her son. I think: It isn't only Mo's son who hides the real self.

"Now how about we get some ice cream?" she says, nodding to the drive-in. "I'm told by that sign that it's real hand-dipped."

And I feel good, because I know this moment isn't about Mo recreating something Eric did in the weeks before he died. Coming to the restaurant and buying ice cream is something between the two of us, Mo and me, a new moment that we're making together. That acting that I did on the set of *Hammered*, pretending I was looking up at the stars, I can see now that it was mostly fake. But I also know that this moment here is as real as it gets.

So I say, "I can't think of anything I'd like better."

Early the next morning, Thursday, we all get breakfast together, then hit the road again.

Russel is driving, and we're almost to the Louisiana border when Mo says, very casually, "Russel, would you mind dropping me off somewhere in Beaumont?"

I turn around and look at her in the backseat. "What?"

"Yeah," she says. "I think I'm going to head north for a bit."

"But—" I start.

She interrupts me, "I just feel like I need to go north now. And you know us aimless drifters."

I stare at her, and she stares back at me, a little smile on her face. And I feel stupid because I knew that Mo was going to leave us at some point, that she wouldn't be going with us all the way to New Orleans. Why would she? She's following Eric's path. So this is the point where her journey heads off in another direction. But I'd already gotten close to her, and part of me wishes she'd given me some kind of advance warning.

I can't say any of this because of Russel. He looks a little surprised, and maybe a little sad, but not that surprised or sad, because he doesn't know what I know. He's already angling the car into the exit.

At the end of the highway exit, Russel pulls into a gas station. There's another road running north.

After Russel and Mo say their goodbyes, she climbs out of the car without even looking me in the eye. I know she wants to talk to me in private, so I say to Russel, "Give me a second."

Out in the parking lot, we stand together shuffling our feet.

"I'm sorry," Mo says. "I should have told you last night."

"No," I say. "It's okay, I understand." I look down at the ground, which is crumbling asphalt. "Thanks for telling me I remind you of your son. I'm really flattered."

She tenderly touches the right side of my face, but it's not like she's touching my scars. It's more like a mother touching her son—like she doesn't even see the scars. And it occurs to me that even now Mo has never commented on or asked me anything about them, and I never told her. In the time I spent with her, I'd mostly forgotten all about them, and I think this might be the first time I can remember that that's ever happened, and it makes me feel even more connected to her.

"Nothing could have made me more proud," she says gently, "than if he'd turned out exactly like you."

"I really hope you find what you're looking for," I say, and at this point, it's hard to hold back my tears.

"And I really hope you get the part," Mo says. "I can't wait to see the movie, because I know you'll be great."

I think: The part! It's another thing I've forgotten about, at least since my conversation with Mo the night before.

Mo and I hug, then with a smile, she turns and walks away. Part of me wants to stop her even now, asking if I can friend her on Facebook, if we can somehow keep in touch, but another part of me knows the time isn't right. Besides, she knows who I am. I'm pretty sure I'll hear from her again eventually.

That's when I realize that Russel has probably been watching all of this from inside the car, and wondering what's going on. So I turn away, trying to dry my eyes without him seeing.

But sure enough, when I get back inside, Russel has a smug little smile on his lips.

"Let's hit the road," I say, trying to preemptively change the subject.

"Hold on," he says.

"What?"

He stares over at me, even as I stay looking out the window. "I have a feeling there was more to her story than I know," he says, "and that I was right about our hitchhiker fitting perfectly into this little road trip adventure of ours."

That's when I realize that Russel really had been right about that—that Mo did have a story to tell, a really interesting one. But I knew then and there that I wasn't going to tell Russel the story, and it wasn't just because he'd be insufferable about it. It was something between Mo and me, and it wasn't any of Russel's business.

"You're crazy," I say, but not loudly, and I don't push the point, because I know I don't have a leg to stand on.

CHAPTER NINE

Back on the road, I feel sad that Mo is gone. Then I spot a pick-up truck that looks like the one that chased us back near Yuma, and I instantly tense.

But no, it's not the same truck at all—this one is dark blue, not black, and the wheels aren't as jacked. So I relax again. A little bit later, we cross the border into Louisiana, and I start to get excited again about the audition. It isn't even ten o'clock yet, and that gives us plenty of time to make it to New Orleans. My appointment with Julian Lockwood isn't until four.

I use my phone to check out the address Greg gave me, the place where the audition is, and I realize it's a residential neighborhood. In other words, I'm pretty sure Julian Lockwood has invited me to some house he owns there.

"We're going to the Garden District," I say to Russel in the driver's seat.

"Really?" he says, perking up

"Yeah," I say. "What? Are you excited because Beyoncé and Jay Z have a house there?"

"Well, it's more the fact that Tiana goes there in *The Princess and the Frog*. But yeah, that works too."

We drive for a second, and Russel fiddles with the air conditioning.

Then he says, "Hey, how did you become an actor anyway? That was after we sort of drifted apart, and I don't think you ever told me."

I know the exact moment I became an actor. But Russel is right that I've never told him the story.

"It all began with my music," I say. "For a few years after my accident, my parents would buy me anything I asked for, to try and cheer me up. And so when I was around twelve, I asked for a guitar. I took lessons and everything, and I really liked it. At this point, my scars were still pretty bad, so no matter what I did, people would praise me. Teachers gave me good grades. I remember one woman stopped me on the street to tell me how much she liked my shoes. She went on and on, and I felt like an idiot, because they were ordinary tennis shoes. Even then, I knew what people were doing, that they were only being nice because they felt sorry for me. But when I would sing and play the guitar for people—family friends, people like that—they complimented me, and for the first time in a long time, I could tell they weren't saying it just to be nice."

"I bet they weren't," Russel says. "You're great."

"Then when I was a senior in high school, I passed the auditorium, and there was a sign out front that said they were holding auditions. It was *King Lear*, and we'd recently read it in class. And I thought, 'Well, they're not going to cast me as King Lear or Edmund, but maybe I could play the Fool.' So I went in, without even really thinking about it. And the director took one look at me, and basically gave me the part then and there. I don't know if you've read the play—"

Russel nods even as he drives. "I have."

"—but it turns out it's actually the perfect role for me. In *Lear*, everything is off about the Fool. He doesn't care how he acts, or how he dresses, or how he looks. The only thing he cares about is telling the truth. He always tells the truth, no matter how harsh or ugly it is."

"But—" Russel starts to say, but I know what he's going to say, so I interrupt.

"I'm not saying I'm ugly," I say. "I am what I am. Like the truth is what it is. It's not good or bad, it just is. The truth is neutral. We're the ones who decide if something is good or bad. It's like my face. And that's the whole point of the Fool, to force King Lear, and maybe the audience, to see things from a different perspective. Do you get it?"

"I do," Russel says quietly. He still looking ahead at the road, but also glancing over at me as much as possible.

"Anyway, the director was really excited about me playing the Fool. And once I realized what we were doing, I was excited too. The designer did this really cool thing with my costume, where everything was divided in half, like my face. It all made sense. But a couple of weeks after rehearsal started, my mom came into my room and sat on the bed, and she asked me, 'Are you absolutely *sure* you want to do this?' And I knew exactly what she was saying: You're going to be up in front of all those people, and they're going to stare at you. She knew how I felt about people staring, especially back then. It's funny because until then I hadn't really thought about that. I'd thought, 'Hey, I like playing my music in front of people, and the director is excited about me playing the Fool.' She was being protective, like any mom. But she really scared me. I started thinking, 'What *am* I doing? Hold the phone here. I'm *literally* stepping into the spotlight!' She saw the panic on my face, and she said, 'It's okay, you don't have to do it. You can pull out even now, and no one's going to judge you.'"

"But you didn't pull out."

I shake my head. "I did think about it, and damn, I was scared. People had stared at me my whole life, and I hated it, and yet here I was, saying to people, 'Come on, stare at me! Don't stop looking.' But then opening night came..."

"And?" Russel says eagerly. "*And?*"

I smile, making Russel squirm a little bit more.

"And it was amazing," I say. "I got a standing ovation—even more applause than the actor playing King Lear. Like, for five minutes. But it wasn't like the lady and my tennis shoes—it wasn't people doing it because they felt sorry for me, to make me feel good. I was good in the role. And people responded. They might not have been able to explain what the director and I were doing, what Shakespeare was doing, but on some level, they got it. We'd shown them something real and profound, something they'd never seen before. We'd made art, and it was beautiful."

"And people were staring, but on your terms," Russel says. "Because you *wanted* them to stare. God, this is so great! If I wasn't driving, I'd be writing this down."

I smile. "I walked onto the stage that night as a clueless high school senior who had no idea what he wanted to do with his life. But being in the spotlight like that felt so completely absolutely right. So I walked off that stage an actor, and I knew I'd spend my whole life doing this—that I'd do whatever it takes to be able to keep doing it."

"And you did! You have. You *are*. Oh, my God, this is giving me chills."

Now I laugh.

"Serious question," Russel says. "Do you think you'd still be an actor if it hadn't been for the accident? Because sometimes I wonder if I'd still be a screenwriter if I wasn't gay—if it hadn't been for all the things that happened to me when I was younger, all the ways that I felt like I couldn't express myself. You know as well as I do how insanely hard it is to make it in the arts, and that the only people who ever do are always the ones who have something to prove."

"It's a good question."

"And? What's your good answer?"

"Well, my first thought is always, 'Hell, yes! Because I'm kind of a ham.' I like applause a lot. People want to take selfies with me? I mean, come on."

"What's your second thought?"

I consider, then say, "That it doesn't matter. We're all the sum total of our experiences. I'm the guy who got his face burned when he was seven years old, and tried to make sense of it by becoming an actor. The guy who didn't get burned, maybe he wouldn't have become an actor, but he also wouldn't be me."

Russel considers this, then he says, "Okay, now you're starting to piss me off."

"Why's that?" I say with a smile.

"Because in this little duo of ours, I'm the one who's supposed to be good with words. I'm the writer, remember? But then here you go off on all these great monologues, and this incredibly insightful knowledge about yourself and the whole human condition. So if you don't mind, would you please start dumbing it the fuck down for the remainder of the trip?"

I laugh again. "I'll see what I can do."

"And in the meantime, I totally need to pee."

We stop at the next rest stop, and we do our business, and I'm feeling pretty good about myself, because in addition to liking being told I'm hot, I also appreciate being told I'm good with words.

But when we go back to the parking lot so we can get back on the road, the car won't start.

"Try it again," Russel says, and I do. Like the half-dozen times before, the car turns over, but it never starts.

I'm beginning to panic. "I've got my audition," I say. It's a little after ten-thirty, and I do quick mental calculation, "I've only got five and a half hours to get to New Orleans!"

But Russel is keeping his cool. "We're going to be okay," he says. "Pop the hood."

I pop the hood, and he climbs out and opens it up, taking a hard look inside.

I join him. "What do you see?"

"Absolutely nothing," he says. "I don't know the first thing about cars."

"Then why did you tell me to pop the hood?!"

"I'm not sure. I figured we should at least look to see if—I don't know!—little green gremlins were dancing around on the engine."

I am so not in the mood to laugh about this, and I'm about to tell Russel that, when he says, "But stay calm. I'll call Triple-A now."

He turns away, stepping up onto the sidewalk to make the call. Meanwhile, I stare at the engine. It's not steaming, but I am. I know Russel is trying to help, but he doesn't understand how important my getting to New Orleans is—how it's about all the things I was telling him ten minutes ago in the car. For him, this has all been a silly road trip.

A few moments later, he returns to me. "They're on their way. In the meantime, let's try to start it again."

It takes a half hour before the tow truck arrives, but at least we're only about ten miles from a town—a place called Bluke, Louisiana.

I ask the tow truck driver which of the three service stations he thinks is best, and he drops us off at that one, even though I know he's probably getting a kick-back. By the time we get there, it's noon, but it's less than three hours to New Orleans, so if the fix isn't too complicated I can still make it to the audition on time.

We wait for the mechanic's report in a dusty little office with ridiculously stale coffee.

"Bluke?" Russel says, leaning in and lowering his voice. "There's really a town named Bluke?"

I don't answer, and I can feel Russel staring at me, probably deciding if he should say something to cheer me up. He doesn't, which is totally the right call.

I'm trying to figure out how annoyed I should be with Russel when the mechanic returns.

We both stand.

"It's the fuel pump," the mechanic says, chewing gum. "It's not a hard fix. But we're going to have to order the part."

"Well, do any of the other—?" I start to say.

He shakes his head. "I called around."

"Well, if you order it—"

"Ten o'clock tomorrow morning at the latest."

I instantly despair. I turn to Russel. "I'll get an Uber. Can you take an Uber that far?"

Russel looks at the mechanic. "He needs to be in New Orleans by four. What's the best way to get there from here?"

The mechanic chews loudly. "No Uber out here. Taxi, I guess. But four o'clock?" He flicks his eyes to the clock on the wall. "There's no way you'll get one out here fast enough."

The world is spinning. Why hadn't I gotten a plane out of San Antonio or Dallas? I need to sit again, but I'm seriously not sure if I can make it to the chair.

The mechanic says, "Do you want us to—?'"

"Yes!" Russel says. "Order the part."

The mechanic leaves, and Russel puts a hand on my shoulder, leading me back to a chair. It actually does steady me a little. Once I'm sitting, Russel puts his hand on my knee, and that helps too.

"Call Fiona," he says to me. "See if she can get the audition moved to tomorrow. Meanwhile, I'm going to see if there's any other way to get to New Orleans on time."

While Russel goes out on his quest, I do call Fiona but get Greg on the phone again. I explain the situation.

"Let me make a call," he says. "I'll call you back."

I wait for Greg, and I wait for Russel, and I'm starting to think I'm losing my mind, because I suddenly want to strangle the Michelin Tire Man.

My phone rings, and I answer it.

"Well, there's good news and bad..." He stops himself. "Oh, hell. Julian says Friday is okay. And can I just say?"

"What?"

"The way he's talking, I'm starting to think this might be the real deal. Julian told me he's watched all your old stuff this week—even the web series. We worked with him once before. Plus, I've heard stories. And he doesn't usually act like this. He usually acts like he's doing an actor a huge favor by casting them in his movie. Which he definitely is. But this time, it's different. I think he's really interested in you."

I don't know what to say to this. I don't want to speak because I'm worried he'll say I misheard him and he didn't say any of the things I heard.

"But..." Greg says.

And I think: I knew it!

"What?" I say. "Just *say* it." At this point, he might as well rip the Band-Aid off.

"Well," Greg says, "you absolutely *have* to be there by one p.m. tomorrow at the very, very latest. They have to make the official offer this week—it's some kind of studio accounting thing. It'll save them a lot of money."

If the car-part isn't delivered until ten a.m. tomorrow, and it takes almost three hours to get to Julian Lockwood's house, that could be cutting it really, really close. I'm tempted to say: "If Julian Lockwood and the studio want me so badly, why aren't they sending a damn car for me?" But I don't say it, because once again I'm not sure I want to know the real answer.

Instead, I say, "I'll be there."

And I know I will be. If the car isn't going to be ready on time, I'll hitchhike like Mo.

* * *

I find Russel outside, and I explain everything.

"That's great!" he says, and I nod, but only once. He keeps staring at me, then says, "Now we should get a motel for the night."

He remembers to go in and give the mechanic our contact info, then we look around for a place to stay. Fortunately, everything is within walking distance in Bluke, Louisiana. It's mostly a collection of gas stations, fast food restaurants, and a truck stop, but there is a small downtown—basically a two-block stretch of old buildings, though most of the storefronts are boarded up.

Russel stops in his tracks, creating a little cloud of dust under his feet. "Oh! I just realized," he says, excited.

I stop too. "What?"

"Don't you see? This is the road trip movie cliché involving car trouble."

I truly don't want to encourage him, but at the same time, I know he has a point: it *does* seem like at some point in every road trip movie, the main characters have car trouble. If I'd remembered that the day before, I might have been more likely to get that plane ticket.

"So..." Russel says, "what's going to happen next?" He scans the area, then announces, "Got it!"

"Got what?" I say.

"Can't you see? Look around."

I don't look around—I roll my eyes. This is totally Russel being Russel.

"Well, *look*. Bluke, Louisiana? Even the name is perfect. Have you ever seen a more miserable, pathetic, beaten-down place in your life?"

I sigh. "No."

"And we're gay."

I look at him as if to say, "So?"

"So haven't you ever seen *The Adventures of Priscilla Queen of the Desert?* Or *To Wong Fu! Thanks for Everything, Julie Newmar?*"

"Those movies are about drag queens, not gay guys."

"Close enough. The point is, a group of...okay, *drag queens*...has car trouble and they have to spend the night in some miserable hell-hole in the middle of nowhere. And as a result of their spunk and creativity, they end up solving everyone's problems, mostly by decking them out in sequins."

I clutch my head. "You're so crazy. Just beyond insane."

"You know what else we need?" Russel says. "To get you laid. Because that's the other thing this road trip movie of ours is missing. A romantic subplot. Seriously, it has no sex whatsoever."

And I don't say anything about that, because the one romantic subplot in the trip so far is my feelings for Russel, and that's something that I sure as hell don't want him knowing anything about.

CHAPTER TEN

We find a motel for the night, and even though I'm still kind of annoyed with Russel over his obsession with road trip movie clichés, I only get us one room.

It's still mid-afternoon, way too early for dinner. As we unpack, I see Russel searching for something, and I assume he's going to call Kevin, so I give him some privacy by going out to wait in the chairs in front of the motel room. For once, they're not the same cheap white plastic chairs the motels always had before. They're those brown metal folding chairs, the kind you see in schools, rusted from the rain.

I realize I've been so caught up in everything that's happened that I've barely checked my social media. When I do, I see that the word's gone out about *Hammered* being canceled, and lots of people are sending me messages of support, including some of the other cast members. That's nice, I think. There seems to be fewer insults and hate too. Could the online trolls already be moving on?

I can't handle a fresh burst of hate right now, so I keep my status as it is.

Russel steps out of the room, joining me in the folding chair next to mine.

"Aren't you going to call Kevin?" I ask.

He shakes his head. "He's got this big deadline tomorrow, so he told me not to call. We texted a bit. He's good."

I nod, and we stare out at the parking lot. An SUV drives in with a car full of screaming kids, and I pray to God that they don't get the room next to ours.

"We'll get you to New Orleans on time," Russel says. "I mean it. I absolutely promise."

"Thanks," I say, grateful.

"Besides, there's a scene in every road trip movie where they always have to resort to some alternative method of transportation to get to their destination."

And I sit there next to him, gritting my teeth and doing my best not to throw him under the wheels of the passing SUV.

Later, we find the motel Laundromat and do our dirty laundry. There's only one working machine, but we don't have that much stuff, so we wash it all together, including Russel's green briefs. It's embarrassing to admit even to myself, but somehow that gives me a little tingle.

After that, Russel and I walk to the nearby truck stop for dinner. Inside, it smells like waffles, even this late in the day, and the booths are made of orange vinyl. It's surprisingly crowded, and the linoleum and wood paneling looks like something from the "small town diner" set on a television show, except no set ever looks this drab.

Before we can say anything, the high school prom queen hostess takes one look at me and says, "It's you! You're the guy from that show!"

"Yeah, it's me," I say, smiling.

"Don't move!" she says, then she turns and heads back toward the kitchen.

She returns a moment later with an older man in a blue, short-sleeve button-down and a clip-on tie. I've seen clothes like this in wardrobe departments, but I didn't think anyone really wore them.

"Well!" he says. "It's really you! Welcome to Suzie's! We're so happy to have you here with us."

I can tell he recognizes me—or has at least been told I'm someone famous—but doesn't know my name, so as I shake his hand, I say, "Otto Digmore. And thank you so much."

"Otto Digmore!" he says, even as he's looking at my scars. "Of course. Well, we're really happy you stopped by. Say, would you mind very much if we took your photo? It's for our Wall of Celebrities." He nods to the wall behind the cash register, where there are three pictures in plastic frames, and they're all really old. One is of Lynda Carter, who played Wonder Woman on a TV show a zillion years ago, one is a kid from *The Cosby Show*, back when he was still a kid on *The Cosby Show*, and the third person is someone I don't recognize—a local newscaster, maybe.

"Sure thing," I say, as cool as always.

In the entryway, I pose with the manager—he stands on my left, of course—and the hostess takes a photo on her cellphone.

"Just one more," she says.

Then, peppering us with questions about why we're in town, she leads us to our seats.

"My friend and I are just passing through," I answer, definitely not wanting to get into the weeds about the audition, not like I did with Mo.

As we take our seats, a few people look my way, but it's a pretty old crowd—mostly actual truck drivers and retirees on the way to see their grandkids—so I can tell they're staring because of my scars, not because I used to be on a television show about horny college students.

As Russel and I settle into our booth, I hear a snippet of the conversation behind me. "They kidnap people, you know," the woman is saying. "They take tourists, and then they don't give them back until their relatives pay thousands of dollars. Even in places like Cancun and Puerto Vallarta! That's why I'd never go. You can't trust anyone down there, not even the police."

"There needs to be a word for anti-Mexican prejudice," Russel says, opening his menu. "You know, like 'homophobia'? Is 'Mexi-phobia' too much like 'Mexi-fries'?"

The booth next to us is silent for a moment, and I wonder if they overheard him like at the gas station in Yuma. But Russel wasn't talking loudly, and a second later, the woman starts chattering on again.

Right then, I sense the busboy watching me, grinning. I can tell he recognizes me from *Hammered*—or maybe the hostess pointed me out. Either way, I smile at him, and he blushes. He's young and Latino—a high school student—and between the grinning and the blushing, he's absolutely adorable.

"To think there was a time I actually liked French fries," Russel is saying. "But after this week, if I never have another French fry, I'll be perfectly fine."

Right then, the waitress appears, and we order our food. Once she's gone, I catch the busboy watching me again.

I nod him over.

He does that cute thing people do in movies, where they act like they're not sure they're the person being nodded at.

But I smile and nod again.

He approaches, cautiously, holding one of those gray plastic bins full of dirty dishes.

"Are you really you?" he says. He reminds me of a puppy sniffing someone he doesn't know.

"I am," I say.

"I can't believe it!" he says. "You're Otto Digmore." He stops. "Hey, what's Javier Gomez like?"

Javier is a Latino cast member on *Hammered*, and his part was even smaller than mine.

"He's really, really smart," I say, which is true. "We used to play chess on the set, but I don't think I ever won a single game."

At this, the busboy beams.

Then he says, "Hey, can I ask you a favor? You can say no if you want to, it's okay."

"Sure thing," I say. "Anything at all. What do you need?"

"Really?"

I nod, preparing myself for another couple selfies, but right then the manager appears.

"Ernesto," he says, "I really think you should leave Mr. Dogmore alone."

"It's fine," I say, selling it, but that doesn't make the manager happy. I wink at Ernesto.

"Ernesto..." the manager says.

"Okay, yeah, all right," Ernesto says, turning away, almost knocking into a passing man.

When he's gone, Russel asks me, "Does that ever get old?"

I consider telling Russel about the complications—people harassing me online and shouting at me in airports, and now even coming to my apartment and splattering wax on my door.

But he and I are having a nice dinner, and I can tell he's trying hard to distract me from my worries about making the audition tomorrow.

So instead I smile and say, "Nope. Never."

Midway through dinner, Russel looks at his glass of wine and says, "This is terrible. It's some of the worst wine I've ever had." He turns toward the kitchen. "Waitress? Another glass!"

We both burst out laughing. There's literally no way that Russel or I can drive tonight, and it's been a long week, so we've been drinking all through dinner—wine for Russel, beer for me.

By the time we're done eating, we're both feeling pretty good. I'm at that perfect point where life is fine, everything is light and easy, but I'm not nearly so drunk that I'm going to be hungover the next day.

It's dark out in the parking lot. As we turn toward our motel, a dingy white van pulls up in front of us.

The doors roll open, and a man jumps out—bulky, with black hair, probably another Latino, but older. Still, it's dark, so I can't quite make out any more than that.

He says something to us in Spanish.

"Sorry," I say. "We don't speak Spanish."

But he doesn't seem to understand—I guess he doesn't speak English. He says something else, slower, but no more understandable because I still don't speak Spanish. Then he gestures to the open door in the side of the van, and talks again.

I turn to Russel, hoping that he can make some sense of this, but he looks as confused as I feel. Then I see another person, behind us. It's another Latino—he must have walked around from the driver's seat. He says something too, gesturing to the van. They both want us to get inside.

"I'm sorry," Russel says, obviously nervous, "but we really don't understand you. And we really need to go now."

Then Russel grabs me by the arm and turns us to one side, trying to walk away.

The first guy steps in front of us, talking fast again, more loudly now.

The guy behind us has moved closer too. He smells like sweat and stale cigarettes. He's holding something on the underside of his wrist, something long and made of metal. A knife? I smell a hint of gasoline now too, and I'm not sure if it's coming from the street or inside the van. Either way, it's making me even more nervous.

"Russel," I say under my breath, "I think he has a knife."

"*What?*" Russel says, and I hear the fear in his voice.

We both look around, but there's no one else outside—there are other cars in the lot, but everyone is inside the restaurant. There aren't even any cars passing out on the street.

The men are both talking now, jabbering in Spanish, stepping closer, penning us in, edging us toward the open doors of the van.

In movies and on TV, whenever someone forces someone else into a van, I always think: *That would never happen to me, I wouldn't allow it!*

But somehow it's not that simple here. I'm scared and confused, and I'm starting to panic, even though I'm not sure if it's because of the vague smell of gasoline or the whole strange situation. I'm also more than a little tipsy, and the guys are babbling in Spanish, and I keep seeing the flash of metal near the one guy's wrist. Everything happens so fast.

"Stop it!" I say, trying to pull away, but then the guys are outright pushing us, and Russel and I are suddenly somehow inside the darkness in the back of the van.

There are no seats, just empty space. It smells like rubber and more stale cigarettes and, yes, that hint of gasoline.

The second the doors slam shut, I remember the words of the woman in the restaurant:

They kidnap people, you know, she'd said. *They take tourists, and then they don't give them back until their relatives pay thousands of dollars.*

But that was just anti-Mexican prejudice. Wasn't it? I know that tourists have been kidnapped in Mexico, but we're not in Mexico. We're in Louisiana.

Maybe these are some of the people who've been harassing me online—maybe someone else in the restaurant recognized me, and they were waiting outside. Or maybe this has to do with the guys who harassed us earlier—the black pick-up truck. This is a different vehicle, and different people too, but maybe those other guys spotted us earlier, and they hired someone to grab us. I'd thought all along that we hadn't seen the last of them.

My head is spinning, and the van jerks into motion. Was the engine running all along? I fumble for something to hold onto, but there isn't anything—just the deep grooves in the metal on the floor. There aren't any windows in the back of the van, but I catch a glimpse of the windows up front, and I only see a dull haze—no neon or streetlights. Is it possible we're already on the outskirts of town. It's true it was pretty small.

Then the van starts bouncing, and I hear something crunching under the tires, and I'm thinking we've left the pavement, that we're now on a gravel backroad. I know that can't possibly be good, so now I really am starting to panic, but it's not a panic attack, at least not like any I've ever had before. Somehow this seems a lot more real than that, like the feelings wouldn't go away even if I had remembered to bring my beta-blockers. I can feel the lump of my phone in my pocket, and I want to reach for it, to try and call 9-1-1. But I know that it will make a glow in the dark, and that might be obvious to the guys in the front seat, including the guy in the passenger seat, the guy with the knife.

Now I smell sweat, along with the stale cigarettes, and rubber, and hint of gasoline, but right away I realize it's not the guys in the front seat I'm smelling—it's me, the scent of my own fear, bursting up out onto my skin in the form of perspiration.

I can barely see Russel in the dark, but I can make out the whites of his eyes, and I can see that he's as scared as I am. I'm still feeling the effects of the beer in the restaurant, dizzy from the rocking of the car and the smear of hazy darkness, but at the same time my brain begins to focus.

I think: We might die tonight. We might die, and Russel would never know about my feelings for him—that I've loved him ever since we first met, even though I'd tried to deny it. That he's the only guy I've ever really loved.

"Russel," I whisper, still clutching the metal grooves in the floor, trying to keep from sliding. "There's something I need to tell you."

Right then, the van jerks to a stop. We haven't even gone five minutes from the restaurant.

It's still dark outside. Somehow I know we're out in the middle of nowhere.

In the front of the van, the doors squeak open and the driver and his friend climb out.

I hold my breath, wondering what's going to happen next.

Then someone yanks the door of the van open, and I stare out into the gloom.

CHAPTER ELEVEN

It takes a second for my eyes to adjust.

Then Ernesto, the busboy from the restaurant, steps in front of the open door with that big, adorable grin on his face. Behind him the two men who brought us here appear, also smiling, like they've done something to be proud of.

Beyond them all is some kind of trailer park—twenty units or so, mostly double-wides—in a big grassy field. And beyond the trailer park, surrounding us, the grass grows tall, up to a person's waist, and I can smell hay on the cool evening breeze, but mostly the air smells fresh and clean. In the distance, insects chirp and buzz.

"You came!" Ernesto says happily. "I can't believe you really came!"

He's talking to me, but Russel and I both stare at the kid, still trying to make sense of everything that's just happened.

Russel and I crawl forward into the light, out of the van, unfolding ourselves, standing upright.

I guess Ernesto can see that we're not happy, because he says, "Is everything okay?"

"We didn't know who these guys were," I say. "Or where they were taking us."

Now I have a clearer sense of the guys who brought us here. They're big all right, but not exactly fit. They also have happy, almost goofy, expressions on their faces. I can see that the one guy doesn't have a knife in his hand: it's a row of decorative metal studs on the sleeve of his denim jacket.

I feel like an idiot. How come I didn't notice any of this before? I'm sure it's partly because Russel and I are kind of drunk, but I know it's also because we'd seen what we expected to see—what we were scared of.

"Didn't they explain...?" Ernesto says. "Mr. Dixon said I couldn't talk to you, and then I needed to come home and get Adriana ready."

"We don't speak Spanish," I say. "And they don't speak English."

"¡No manches!" Ernesto says, his face falling, and I have to admit he looks adorable even now, so it's hard to be too mad, especially since I now know I'm not going to die tonight.

He turns to his friends and starts talking to them in Spanish. The longer he goes on, the more angry he sounds, and the more embarrassed his friends look, even though he's a lot younger than they are.

All this does make me feel a little better. I'm finally starting to relax.

After his friends skulk away, I say to Ernesto, "What did you want? Why did you bring us all the way out here?"

"I wanted you to meet my sister," he says quietly. "We watch your show together. I asked you at the restaurant?"

"You didn't ask..."

But when I think back, I remember that he *had* asked me in the restaurant if I'd do him a favor. And I'd said, "Sure thing," like I always do. I may have even added, "Anything at all." I'd thought he was talking about taking a selfie with me, but now I see that wasn't what he meant.

"Your sister?" I say.

"I knew she'd go crazy," Ernesto says. "But it was hard to get her to the restaurant. She has cerebral palsy."

I look over at Russel, and see the expression on his face, and I know that he's feeling the same things I am—mostly stupid, and a little bad.

"Are you mad?" Ernesto says. "Does that mean you won't see her?"

And I smile and say, "I'd love to meet your sister."

Inside the nearest mobile home, I meet Adriana, who looks about twelve years old, but I learn later is actually sixteen. She's in a wheelchair, and her body is a bit contorted, twisted to one side. She has a ribbon in her hair, and she's wearing a simple blue dress. She smells good too, like she's just out of the shower, and I'm pretty sure that this is all for my benefit—that Ernesto told his family I was coming, and she's spent some time getting ready.

Celebrities do a lot of meet-and-greets—mostly contest winners and the children of executives, but also a lot of disabled kids. Once we had this Make-a-Wish kid with leukemia come to the set of *Hammered* to meet Arvin Mason. Beforehand a publicist pulled me aside and said, "Just talk to him like he's totally normal." I guess she'd forgotten who I was, that I consider myself disabled too, and that I worked with disabled kids long before *Hammered*. So it was sort of fun to be able to say, "*Like* he's normal, huh?" She was really embarrassed and apologetic, which was fine with me. I know that most people don't mean to be insensitive clods, but that doesn't make it any easier when they are.

I step forward toward Adriana and sink down to her eye-level. "Hi, there," I say. "I'm Otto Digmore. Ernesto tells me that you and he watch my TV show."

She's obviously overwhelmed, like she can't believe this is happening. At this point, I'm not sure if Adriana is able to talk, or if she even speaks English. But I decide to keep talking for the time being.

"Oh, no," I say. "You thought Ernesto was lying, didn't you? That I wasn't coming? Well, I don't blame you. I mean, look at those shifty eyes."

At this, I glance over at Ernesto, standing in the corner, and he's positively beaming.

Adriana laughs, and now I know she understands English.

"I didn't think he was lying," she says. It's a little difficult to understand what she's saying because her speech is labored, but it's not that bad.

"No?" I say. "He's a pretty good brother then?"

Adriana nods happily. There are other people around us too, Adriana's mother and father, and I think about how hard it must be for Adriana, living with all these people inside this small house. There was a homemade wheelchair ramp at the front door, but even so, I wonder how often she gets to leave.

"So you watch *Hammered*, huh?" I ask, and she nods. "You know what's funny? I'm *in* the show, but I haven't even seen a lot of the episodes. What do you like about it?"

"Dustin," she says with a smile.

Dustin is my character, so I say, "You're just saying that." But then with pretty good comic timing, I grin and lean in closer and say, "Go *ooooon*."

She laughs and says, "I like that he sticks up for himself. And that everyone likes him."

I think: She obviously sees herself in my character, she's living a little vicariously through him. Maybe Dustin being accepted by the group gives her some hope about her own future. As we talk, it's hard not to feel kind of good about the world, about how it's changing for the better in at least *some* ways, like visibility for people like us. But mostly I feel good for Adriana, because I'm pretty sure that my visiting her is one of the best things that's happened to her in a while.

We talk a bit more about the show, and also a new show called *Speechless*, which has a character with cerebral palsy played by an actor who actually has cerebral palsy. Adriana's parents still smile, but they're also hovering. I don't mind that they're taking pictures, but all the people, and the fact that the trailer is so small, is making me feel claustrophobic.

Which is why I'm glad when Ernesto says, "Hey, why don't we go outside? There's a fire pit." He looks at Russel and me. "Can you guys stay a little longer?

I exchange a glance with Russel, who smiles and says, "Sure."

There's a little fire pit in an open area in the middle of the trailer park. Ernesto gathers some wood and lights it, and the four of us—Ernesto, Russel, me, and Adriana in her wheelchair—all sit around it, watching the flames flicker in the night. Adriana's parents get the message to stay away, but once or twice, I see them watching from afar.

The fire flickers lazily, and we're still far from any city lights, and the stars blaze overhead, so the night suddenly feels a little bit like something out of a dream.

"Adriana has a YouTube channel," Ernesto tells Russel and me.

"Really?" I say. "That's great." I look at her. "Can I see? What's it about?"

"My life," she says as Ernesto cues it up on his phone. "And the things I like on TV."

Russel and I watch a couple of the videos, and it's amateurish, but Adriana is surprisingly charming.

"It's great!" Russel says, and I emphatically agree.

"I don't have very many subscribers," she says.

"That's okay," I say. "At least you're the star of the show, right? On *Hammered*, I was only a supporting character, so I barely got any screen time at all." My Pepsi is empty, so I suddenly crush the aluminum can in my hand. "Not that I *miiiind*!" I say maniacally, really trying to sell it.

I know I'm performing for the crowd, but it's what they expect. Besides, I'm an actor, and this is what I do.

"Can I ask something?" Ernesto says to me.

"Shoot," I say.

"Would you rather be a supporting actor in a great show, or the star of one that's just okay?"

I'm afraid to ask Ernesto which he thinks *Hammered* is—a great show or a so-so one—but I have a feeling I already know.

But Russel immediately perks up in his seat. "Oh, man, that's a *great* question. The Ana Ortiz Conundrum."

"What?" I say. "Who's Ana Ortiz?" I really don't know the name.

"*Ugly Betty!*" Adriana says happily.

And Ernesto nods. "Ana Ortiz was Hilda, Betty's sister, on *Ugly Betty.*"

"Which was a *great* show," Russel says. "But she was also the star of this other show, *Devious Maids*, which was terrible."

I don't know either show, but Ernesto and Adriana laugh and seem to be agreeing with Russel.

"So," Russel goes on, "would you rather be like Ana Ortiz on *Ugly Betty*—a small part on a great show—or Ana Ortiz on *Devious Maids*—a big part on a shitty show?"

This really is a good question, and it's not one I've specifically thought about before. I think about it now, even as everyone watches me.

Finally, I say, "It's harder to answer than you'd think. And it's not because we actors are all self-absorbed hams. Well, it's not *just* that. On one hand, you want your work to be seen, you want to be part of something real and special and lasting. So you think, oh, yeah, *Ugly Betty* all the way. On the other hand, most supporting parts really kind of suck. Every now and then they're good, like the Fool in *King Lear*. But most of the time, they're boring. Simple. There's nothing challenging or interesting for the actor. Dustin had, like, three storylines the whole season. And I like that people like him"—at this I smile at Adriana—"but he's always sort of this nice, saintly, straightforward guy. Kind of boring, at least to play. Even the Fool, he doesn't really have an arc—he doesn't really change in any way. Most of the time, the supporting character is only there to serve some plot function for the main character."

"But you have to pick," Ernesto says.

"Yeah!" Russel says. "Supporting actor in a piece of art, or leading actor in a piece of shit."

"But I *can't* choose," I say, clawing at my face and using a funny British accent. "I just can't *do* it."

Everyone laughs. This whole conversation is making me like Adriana and Ernesto. I'm realizing that, in addition to being adorable, Ernesto is also smart and thoughtful and considerate. Which, of course, makes me wonder if he might be gay. But I don't say that.

Instead, I ask him, "Ernesto, what do you want to do with your life?"

"College," Adriana says. "He wants to go to college."

"Oh?" Russel says, and I wonder if he's thinking the same thing I am about Ernesto being gay.

"Well, *Hammered* makes it look pretty great," he says with a grin.

I'm tempted to tell Ernesto that college isn't really anything like it is in *Hammered*, but I decide he's smart enough to understand that it's only a TV show. And I kind of like the idea of Russel hearing that this show he thinks is so bad—that *everyone* thinks is so bad—is actually pretty inspirational to people like Ernesto and Adriana.

"But I can't," Ernesto goes on.

"Yes, you *can*," Adriana says, shaking her wheelchair she's so annoyed.

"What?" Russel asks her.

"He thinks he needs to help take care of me," she says. "He thinks if he goes away, I'll be lonely."

"Will you be?"

"Who *cares*? Even if I am, I'll feel worse if he doesn't do what he wants because he's worried about *me*." She's still rocking her wheelchair.

"It's not that easy," Ernesto says. "For one thing, I probably won't get in. And we can't afford it."

"How are your grades?" I ask.

"They're *good*," Adriana says.

"You know, I could write you a letter of recommendation," I say. "I don't know if it'll make a difference, their getting a letter from me. But it might. And you and Adriana could make a video application. I hate to tell you guys to play the cerebral palsy card, but—"

"Yes!" Adriana says, her eyes shining. "Let's play the cerebral palsy card! Darn right we will."

"But..." Ernesto says.

"And how about I tweet about Adriana's YouTube channel?" I open my phone and punch up a few screens. "Look, I'm doing it now, telling people to subscribe. I know that online friends aren't the same thing as real friends, but it's a start, right?" I glance over at her. "I bet you can make some real connections. I'll even see if I can connect you up with Micah Fowler." This is the actor with cerebral palsy on *Speechless*. I've never met him, but I know how incredibly easy it is for one celebrity to contact another one. "But I do get harassed on social media from time to time, so if anyone gives you crap, ignore them, okay? It's the downside to being popular on Twitter, and also being different in any way." I check Adriana's YouTube channel. "Look, you already have forty new subscribers."

Ernesto shows her the screen, and she squeals a bit, and I feel pretty good. My social media presence—my having seven hundred thousand followers on Twitter—has mostly caused me nothing but misery these past few months. So why not use it for something good for a change?

But I see Russel looking at me with a stupid smile on his face, and I remember what he said about this little town being like something out of *Priscilla Queen of the Desert* and *To Wong Fu! Thanks for Everything, Julie Newmar*. He said that he and I, two gay guys, were going to sweep into town and magically solve everyone's problems.

And I know that, at least from Russel's crazy point of view, that's exactly what we just did.

We stay a bit longer after that, then say our heartfelt goodbyes, and also connect with each other on Facebook. Ernesto has his friends drop Russel and me off back at our motel.

As I'm unlocking our motel room, Russel says to me, "Well? *Well?*"

"Don't say it," I say. "Don't even say it."

"How can I *not* say it?" he says. "I was totally right about this town! Everything that happened tonight, it was right out of a movie."

"Was not."

"It was! What you did for Ernesto and Adriana? You ended up turning their lives around."

"I tweeted out a link, and I offered to write a letter of recommendation."

Russel glares at me.

"Okay, okay," I say. "You were right, okay?" What happened this evening wasn't really anything like the road trip movie cliché, but it was close enough that I know if I don't admit it, Russel is never going to let it rest.

"Which reminds me," Russel says drolly, "what are the odds that Ernesto isn't gay?"

I smile. "You thought so too?"

"Are you kidding? Smart, considerate, devoted to his sister. And so adorable."

"Yeah, that's exactly the word I was thinking— adorable."

"He's like liquid cuteness. You want to rub him into your skin and use him as a moisturizer. And give him a few years...oh, man."

Together we laugh, and it's breezy and intimate, and I can't help but think that this feels like a conversation two boyfriends would have—two people who were part of a couple, coming home after some social event together.

I like it. Is this what it would feel like if Russel and I were a couple? Laughing and unwinding together, sharing secret thoughts, maybe even inappropriate ones that we'd never tell another living soul?

I move to the sink, and he sits on the bed, which sags badly.

"But there's something I still want to know," he says.

"What's that?" I say, brushing my teeth, expecting him to say something else about Ernesto.

Then Russel says, "In the van, when we both thought we might die, you said there was something you wanted to tell me. What was it?"

CHAPTER TWELVE

It's a good thing I've got a mouthful of toothpaste, because I can pretend like I can't talk because I'm brushing my teeth. But I think: What am I going to say when I finally spit? I can't tell Russel what I was really going to tell him—that I still have feelings for him. It would ruin everything.

In the reflection in the mirror above the sink, I can see Russel behind me, sitting on the bed, staring at me.

Finally, I spit out the toothpaste and go to great lengths to rinse out my mouth.

Then I turn to face him and say, "I wanted to thank you."

"For what?" he says.

My eyes scan the ugly yellow carpet under my feet. "For coming with me this week. Getting the part in this movie, it's so important to me right now. Maybe it's stupid. Maybe I'm doing that thing that people do where they tell themselves they'll finally be happy if they get this one more thing, but then they never *are* happy. I mean, I got cast on an actual TV show. And now I want more: Okay, yes, I got cast on a TV show, but now please let me be cast in this feature film. But I don't think that's what this is. More than anything, I

157

want to be an actor. *Hammered* got me some attention, but it wasn't really about my acting. And now that the show is over, it seems like my whole career is already over. I don't want to spend the rest of my life playing horrible, retrograde parts like Freddy Krueger in *A Nightmare on Elm Street*. More than anything in the world, I want to show the world what I can do. That's what happened in that production of *King Lear* back in high school—I made magic. That's the reason I went into acting in the first place. Since I came to Hollywood, I've made money, but I haven't made magic. And that's what I really want to do."

I look up at last, squarely facing Russel. "Anyway," I finish, "thanks for helping me get a chance to do that. That's what I wanted to say."

None of this is really what I wanted to tell Russel in that van, obviously. It's all still true, but it's mostly a stream of random thoughts.

Still on the bed, Russel thinks, then nods. "Well, you're welcome. I get it, I really do."

He squirms a little, and the bed squeaks.

"What?" I say.

"Huh?" he says. "Oh. Well, when I thought we might die, I wanted to say something to you too."

The bed squeaks again.

"You did?" It's hard not to get excited about this. Did Russel want to tell me what I'd wanted to tell him—that he's loved me ever since we met, that I'm the only guy he's ever really loved?

"I wanted to apologize," he says.

"For what?" I say.

"Well, this is awkward after everything you just said. But this week, I've been jealous of you. Otto, the truth is, I'm so happy for you, for all your success. I really,

really am. No one deserves it more than you. And most of the time, that's all I ever think. But this whole trip, I've kept thinking, 'You're going to go to an audition with Julian Lockwood. You might get to be the *lead* in a Julian Lockwood movie.' And I think that's so fantastic, and I'm really happy for you. But lately it also reminds me how pathetic my career is right now. So I've been feeling jealous."

This isn't what I wanted Russel to say. Hearing it when I was expecting something else—namely, that he still loves me—breaks my heart a little. It's even worse because I can tell it's the truth. Russel told me the truth, but I didn't have the guts to say the same thing to him. Then again, what would be the point? We're *not* going to die. And Russel is with Kevin now—they love each other—and the last thing in the world I want to do is come between the two of them.

Russel is staring at me, and I know I have to say something, even if my heart is still broken a little.

I take a seat next to him on the bed—close enough to be intimate, not close enough to be creepy. Also, I've just brushed my teeth, so I know I don't have to worry about bad breath.

"It's going to happen for you too," I say. "It *is*. You're really talented. And I don't know anyone who loves movies more than you do. If you don't get to make movies, there's something really wrong in the world. I haven't been in Hollywood that long, but I've been there long enough to know that talent matters. Hype and buzz, and wearing the right shoes, and being really hot and having sex with the right people—they all matter too. But talent does matter some. And you have it. It's only a matter of time before someone else sees that."

He arches his back a little, like he's pleased with what I've told him. "Really?"

"Really."

Our eyes meet, and it's definitely a "moment," and there's electricity between us. And even now, part of me is hoping that Russel will lean forward and hug me, and maybe kiss me in a way that could maybe lead to something more. But another part of me knows that won't happen, and doesn't *want* it to happen.

But to make absolutely sure it doesn't happen, I stand up and walk to the sink again, to wash my face before bed.

The next morning, Russel is up even before I am, showering and getting ready to leave. He's already gone out and got breakfast—some bananas and muffins from a mini-mart, probably.

When he steps out of the bathroom, he says, "I figured they might get the part for the car early, so we might as well be at the service station, ready to go."

I'm impressed he's being so thoughtful.

And sure enough, the part *was* delivered early. When we get to the gas station a little before nine, the mechanic says they should be done any minute.

By nine-thirty, we're on the road again, and it looks like I won't have any problem making it to New Orleans for my one o'clock audition with Julian Lockwood.

*   *   *

The closer we get to New Orleans, the worse the traffic gets, but it's still nothing like Los Angeles. Sometimes we have to slow down a bit, but it's never even close to feeling like a monster truck rally.

And before we know it, we're in the Garden District, which is this historical district made of old mansions. The streets are lined with big, stately trees, and the yards are clean and manicured—all the green is probably why it's called the Garden District. As for the mansions, a lot of them are former plantations, so they have these big columns like something out of Ancient Greece. But the lots have all been subdivided, and now there are other mansions around them too—Victorians and Italian villas. What they mostly have in common is the fact that they're very old. The elevation here is a little higher than the rest of the city, especially the poor areas like the Lower Ninth Ward, so nothing was flooded during Hurricane Katrina back in 2005.

I'm driving, and Russel is navigating on his phone, and before long, we're parked on the street outside Julian Lockwood's mansion, which is one of the biggest and nicest ones we've seen so far. It gleams a bright white, but it's the American South, so it somehow feels a little dirty too, like the white paint is trying to cover up something unseemly.

It's a little after twelve.

"We really made it," I say.

"I told you we would," Russel says, smiling.

We both read our phones for a while, but I'm too distracted to concentrate, even to notice if people are harassing me on social media. At twelve-forty-five, I step out of the car. We have no idea how long the audition will take, and it seems silly to leave Russel in the car, so he comes with me.

I open the gate in the squeaky wrought-iron fence, then we walk up to the front porch.

It's like I can feel the strain of the big white pillars around me, desperate to hold up this old house, or maybe it's only my own nervousness. Clutching the script in one hand, I ring the doorbell, thinking: This is it, the point of no return. But then I remember: I'm right for this part. And it's not just me—everyone at that other audition thought so. Either Julian Lockwood will agree, or he won't, so I might as well get it over with.

The door opens. I'm expecting a personal assistant, or maybe even a butler in a tuxedo given the way the houses look around us. But no, it's Julian Lockwood himself.

He's older, in his sixties probably, but he has the weirdly timeless air about him that a lot of people in Hollywood have—whether as a result of wheat grass and working out, or botox and fillers. He's tall and lean with stringy brown hair and something of a beak for a nose. But his green eyes are friendly and wise.

When he sees me, something happens to those eyes. They light up, I think.

"Otto Digmore," he says in an English accent. "You made it. Please, come inside."

"Thanks, Mr. Lockwood."

"Please call me Julian."

Julian Lockwood wants me to call him Julian. *And* his eyes seemed to light up. I'm so excited it's hard not to explode like one of those little plastic champagne bottles with the firecracker that spews out paper streamers.

I introduce Julian to Russel, and they shake hands. The house is massive inside, and decorated with a lot of class, almost like a movie set. There's a little table in the middle of the entry hall displaying a vase with a big beautiful bouquet of fresh-cut flowers. I think: Is he so rich that he's one of those people where someone comes in every week even when he's not here, to replace the flowers and clean the house in case he might stop by?

The mansion is so still that somehow I know the three of us are the only ones here. I'm wondering where Julian Lockwood's assistant is, but I don't dare ask. The house smells like Cajun spices from the kitchen, and fresh-cut flowers, and a touch of dust.

"This is a fantastic place," I say.

"Thank you, it's my little home away from home," Julian Lockwood says, sounding exactly like the rich, elitist Hollywood director you'd expect.

I know I should make more small talk, that this first kind of acting is still a really important part of the audition—maybe now even more than usual. But it's like I've come to the doctor's office for the results of some cancer test, and I desperately want to get it over, to learn what I came here to learn. I also want to show Julian Lockwood what I can do with this damn part.

"I can't believe you drove all this way," he says. "Can I get you something to drink? Or maybe some lunch?"

I say no, that's all right. Russel takes the cue from me, and says he's doesn't want anything either.

"Okay, then," Julian Lockwood says, "why don't we get started?" He points to a room on the far side of the entryway. "Russel, would you like to wait in the library while Otto and I go into the parlor?"

And we all do a little dance, maneuvering our way around into the different rooms, and then it's me and Julian Lockwood, alone in the parlor, which has a high ceiling and stark white walls, and more fresh-cut flowers. There's a pair of women's flats near the doorway into the kitchen.

"I just want to say how much I love the script," I say. "And I *know* everyone says that, but I really do. Especially the ending. I love it."

Julian Lockwood smiles, beaming. "Yes, I think we've finally got it where we want it to be, don't we?"

I'm tempted to add how I think I can really bring something to the role of Zach—not just my acting, but my face. But I figure that's got to be obvious, especially for someone as smart as Julian Lockwood, who's probably been working on the script for years.

"Could I get you to read the cocktail party monologue?" he asks me.

"Sure thing," I say. This is the scene I read before, but I've always had a knack for memorizing things, and I'm already off-book just from reading the script over and over these past few days. I don't even bother opening it. Instead, I put it on the end table.

Then I do the lines.

And I'm good. I'm probably not quite as good as I was on Monday, because I'm auditioning for Julian flippin' Lockwood. But I still know I'm good. I really want to say, "Can I do another scene?" because I feel like I'm not quite there, but I don't say anything, because asking for another scene is totally the director's prerogative.

But I'm dying to know what he's thinking.

"That was really nice," Julian Lockwood says, smiling, but that doesn't tell me much because that's what a director would always say, especially if you've come halfway across the country for the audition.

He pages through his copy of the script, his eyes scanning the words. But I'm trying to read *him*. At every audition I've ever done, I always had a sense of how I was doing. Sometimes I was a little off, sometimes I didn't get parts that I thought I would, but I always had some kind of sense.

But this is like the audition in Century City: I have no idea what Julian Lockwood is thinking. Then again, this *is* Julian Lockwood, and maybe he's trying to keep me on my toes. On *Hammered*, I noticed that the really good directors are usually pretty good actors themselves. They know how to project exactly the expressions they want on their own faces, to give the actors a feeling of confidence, or maybe instill a bit of fear. In this case, maybe he's still distracted by his "family emergency"—whatever it is.

The director looks up at last. "Shall we do another scene? How about the park scene on page forty-two? The conversation between Zach and Maggie. I'll read Maggie."

Of course I've also got this scene memorized. But I'm impressed with Julian Lockwood because this is an unusual scene for an audition—subtle, not big and showy. It's also a good scene for me, because if they do decide to cast me, a guy with scars on his face, this is one of the scenes where they would be the most effective.

We read the scene together. I still don't look at the script, which I hope impresses him.

This time, I nail it. I'm present, in the moment. I *am* Zach, connecting with Maggie, existing in a completely different space and time.

I break, returning to Julian Lockwood's house in the Garden District.

The director hesitates. If anything, he seems even less enthusiastic about me now than he did after the cocktail party monologue. Or torn, anyway. But I know I nailed the scene, much better than before.

Something is going on, something I don't understand. It's like that first audition, except maybe even weirder.

"One more, shall we?" Julian Lockwood says. "How about the scene at the factory?"

I ignore him. Instead, I take the seat across from him. The velvet padding is surprisingly hard.

"What's going on?" I say. I don't know why I'm asking him, being so direct like this, but somehow I can't seem to help myself.

"Pardon me?"

Finally, I say, very quietly, "I didn't get the part. Did I?" I don't know how I know this, but I do.

"What in the world makes you say that?" he says, and for a second I worry that I've made a huge mistake, stopping the audition like this. Julian Lockwood is definitely a good actor because he really does seem surprised by my question. There's an acting expression that good acting is reacting—that the hardest part of acting is really listening to the other actor, and making your reaction to the words they're saying as real and genuine as the words *you're* saying.

But acting is what I do for a living. I know the craft pretty well. So I can tell when even someone as good as Julian Lockwood is doing it wrong.

"Just tell me the truth," I say.

He stares at me, and this time his eyes definitely light up, even more than before. But now there's something forlorn about them too.

Then, as quietly as me, he says, "No, you didn't get the part."

I expect to feel the world crashing down around me, or maybe a hurricane like Katrina blowing through the house, knocking out the windows. But the house is as still and quiet as always. As for me, I don't feel much of anything.

"It had already been decided, hadn't it?" I say. "Before I even read?"

Julian nods sadly. He's not acting now—I can tell. This is the real deal.

"The studio made the decision last night," he says. "They've put in an offer to Miles Teller, and he accepted this morning."

"He'll be great," I say, nodding. It's exactly who I expected them to cast. "But..."

"Why did I let you read?"

I nod.

"Because I know you came all this way," he says. "And because I could tell you wanted it so badly."

So this was nothing more than another courtesy read. But somehow I know there's something else he's not saying. Once again, his acting isn't good enough to hide it. So I say that: "There's more."

He smiles now, but it's a sad smile too.

"Just tell me," I say. "Please."

"Okay." He inhales, holds it. "I *was* interested in you. Very interested. I've been watching videos of your work all week, and I think you'd be terrific in the role. It's a good script, yes, especially the ending, and I hope the movie will be good too. But with you..." He smiles. "It's not just your face, your scars. I have a feeling you've *lived* this script. That you could bring a level of realism, of truthfulness, that you don't see in the movies very often. Ever since I got a sense of your passion, that you were willing to drive all the way out here to see me, I've been fighting for you. 'At least let me read him,' I said. 'If he's good, and I like him, let me at least do a screen test.' But the studio..."

"Says I'm too different," I finish.

Julian nods. "It's partly your low profile—no film credits."

"Partly? What's the other part?"

He hesitates again, but I know what he's thinking.

"My face," I say.

He nods. "They say it's too much of a risk. They feel like the script is already a very big risk for them. Which it is. A love story with an ambiguous ending? If we don't get everything exactly right, this project will bomb. Even if we *do* get it right, it might bomb."

So what Russel had said earlier in the week was right: You can have one different thing in your movie, but you can't have two. And even that one thing can't be *too* different.

"But you're Julian Lockwood," I say. "You won an Oscar."

"But even Julian Lockwood has to choose his battles. So I guess what I really wanted was for you to come here today and read—"

"—and fail," I finish.

He nods. "I wanted to be wrong about you. I wanted you to come here, and I'd find out that you were an interesting idea, but you were ultimately wrong for the part. That you didn't have the chops."

"But I do."

"Yes, you do. I think you could be terrific in this movie, and if it were only up to me, I would at least test you. But it's not only up to me, and the decision's been made. There's nothing I can do except to say I'm really sorry."

I have no idea what to say to that, or even what to do with my hands. So I stand. There is still no big hurricane bearing down on me, nothing to knock me off my feet, but somehow I can tell there is one gathering somewhere nearby, and when it hits, it'll be big. I'm already feeling dizzy from the pressure.

Then I feel myself moving, leaving the room, and somehow I find myself out in the entryway with all the flowers. They stink. So do the spices from the kitchen. How did I not notice this before?

The door opens from the library, and Russel appears—he must have heard my feet on the old floorboards. I can tell he's about to ask me how it went, but then he sees my face, and he knows exactly how it went.

He immediately steps forward and hugs me. "It's okay," he whispers.

Now the floorboards creak behind me—Julian in the open doorway.

"Do you boys have a place to stay?" he says.

I can't seem to answer, so Russel says, "We were going to get a hotel."

"Stay here," Julian says gently. "I feel terrible about this, and it's the least I can do. The house is empty, and I'll be out until very late. Sleep anywhere except the master. Stay the whole weekend if you like—I'll hardly be here."

Russel pulls back, asking me a question with his eyes.

But I can't answer because Hurricane Julian has finally hit, and it's currently tearing through me, destroying everything in its path, and I wonder if there'll be anything at all left behind when it's gone.

CHAPTER THIRTEEN

It's like I'm a wind tunnel, and there's nothing inside me except a wash of dark emotion—resentment, fear, but mostly anger.

But on the outside, I try to keep it together. On the outside, I still look like a person.

It's a few hours later, and we're still in the city of New Orleans, still in Julian Lockwood's house. The director had to leave right after the audition, and he said he'd be gone for the night, but he gave us the combo to unlock the side door.

I've spent the afternoon in a total funk, no matter how hard Russel has tried to console me.

"Shall we get some dinner?" he says at last, still trying to cheer me up.

I've never been in New Orleans before. Even so, the last thing in the world I want to do is go out on the town.

Finally, Russel says, "How about we order a pizza?" and I nod, so that's what we do, eating it in front of the TV, in a den in the back of the house.

As the light from the television flickers on my face like some kind of brain scanner, I can sense Russel looking over at me, again and again. I know he's wondering about me, on the verge of asking me if I'm okay. But I also think I'm scaring him a bit, the way even the non-scarred side of my face isn't registering any emotion at all, and he ends up not saying anything.

It's barely eight o'clock when I say, "I'm going to go to bed."

"Really?" he says. "You don't want to...?"

I turn to look at him. "What?" I say, defying him to suggest something.

"Nothing," he says. He forces out a smile. "Get some sleep, okay?"

Julian Lockwood's mansion has lots of extra rooms upstairs, so there's no point in Russel and me sleeping in the same bedroom tonight. It's the first time we'll be in different bedrooms since the start of the trip, and somehow that makes the emotions in the wind tunnel of my body blow even stronger.

Inside the bedroom, I make the mistake of checking my various online profiles, and I see the haters are back in full force.

Hey Freak! Your dumb-ass show got canceled!
Won't have to look at your UGLY FACE anymore!

Did I really think it would stop because my show had been canceled? I understand now that it will never stop, that decades from now, when I move into a retirement home, people will still be sending me horrible messages online, and splashing candle wax onto my door.

I hear Russel's footsteps in the hallway outside, the floorboards creaking. The ceilings of Julian Lockwood's mansion are high, even upstairs, so sounds echo. Also, none of the doors fit exactly right.

A few minutes later, Russel calls Kevin, and I hear his voice too, more clearly than I ever did on those nights in the motels on the road. It sounds like he's right out in the hall, even though I know he must be in one of the other bedrooms. It's partly because the house is still so quiet.

"I've never seen him like this before," Russel is saying. "I want to help him, but I have no idea how."

Of course he's talking about me, how pathetic I am.

At the same time, they don't talk about me very long. A minute later, they're talking about Kevin's job, about all the other, more important things that are going on in their lives.

Then Russel says, "I love you so much. Two weeks ago, at our wedding, I didn't think it was possible to love you more than I did then. But being away from you, even for a few days, has made me love you even more than that."

And then the wind tunnel that is me shatters, and for the first time since I was an overwrought teenager, I start to cry. My eyes drip with tears, and the sobs explode out of me, and I bury my face in my pillow, hoping that Russel can't hear me the way I can so perfectly hear him.

It's one of those nights where you think you never really fell asleep, but at some point, you look at the clock, and you see it's morning.

I feel like shit, of course. Or maybe it's like I'm made of concrete, and gravity is even stronger than usual. There's no possible way I can get out of bed, except I have to pee. I can feel it hot and burning inside me.

There's a knock on my door, but I don't say anything.

"You okay?" Russel asks, opening the door and gently stepping inside.

"Yeah," I say, but my voice is flat again. I stare at the ceiling.

He shuffles deeper inside, closing the door behind him. I'm so unbelievably tired of the floorboards creaking.

"Did you sleep okay?" he asks.

I know I should move—look over at him, or at least get up and go pee. But I don't.

"Fine," I say.

"You want some breakfast? I can bring something up."

"No."

Russel lingers, halfway between the door and the bed, like he's trying to decide if he should come or go. We still haven't talked about when we're heading back to Los Angeles, but I'm hoping he doesn't ask me anything about it now, because somehow it seems like the most difficult question in the world to answer.

Still more fucking creaks—Russel coming toward me. I feel the bed droop—he's sitting at the end of my bed now. But it's a big bed, so he's still pretty far away.

"This so sucks," he says. "I can't believe this. Especially after we came all this way. This isn't a very good ending at all."

I still don't move, just keep staring up at the ceiling, feeling like a concrete statue that desperately needs to pee. But finally I look down at him sitting on my bed. He's wearing his cargo shorts again, and I can't believe how much that bugs me.

"A good ending?" I say quietly.

"You know," he says, "for our road trip movie." He thinks for a second, then leans backward on the bed, propping himself upright with his hands. He half-smiles, sort of casually. "Except maybe it sort of figures when you think about it. This is even kind of another road trip movie cliché. Wherever they're going, it's never what they expect. *Vacation. Little Miss Sunshine. The Wizard of Oz.* Even *Zombieland.* That's the whole point, I guess. They set out on a journey wanting to get somewhere really bad, but when they get there, it isn't what they thought it would be. But it doesn't matter because they've realized something about themselves, something important and unexpected—something they never would have known if they'd never left in the first place." He grins outright now, ironic, but also gentle and disarming. "So what did *you* learn? What's the real reason we came all this way?"

And at this, something in me snaps.

I sit upright in bed. "This isn't a fucking road trip movie," I say. "This is my fucking *life!*"

Russel immediately wilts. "I know that. Oh, God, Otto, I'm sorry! I was just being silly. I was trying to cheer you up. But it was stupid. Oh, my God, I can't believe I said all that. I honestly wasn't trying to make fun of you. I know this isn't a movie. I know this is your real life."

"You don't know..." I say. "You can't understand how hard this is."

"You're right. But I can imagine."

"How? *How* can you imagine? You *can't!*"

Russel pulls back, shrinking farther, even as he stays sitting on the bed.

And suddenly everything crashes in on me again. My whole life, it's always been the same: no matter what happens, it always ends in disappointment. I spend my twenties taking shit roles, playing outcasts and zombies, and then I finally land a job on a sitcom, finally get some attention for myself, but it ends up being another excuse for people to stare at me, and call me a freak in ways that are even worse than back in grade school. And then it's canceled after a few months anyway.

Then I hear about this role in a movie—a really great role, perfect for me—and I drive all the way to New Orleans to read for it, but that's a big bust too. It would have been one thing if I'd never heard of this role at all, or if I'd done the audition, and then they'd said, "Nah, we don't think you're right for the part." Or even, "Sorry, but you weren't very good." But I *was* right for the part, and I was good too, and everyone knew it, and they told me so to my face. Julian Lockwood, the Goddamn Oscar-winning director, said I'd "lived" the part. So do I get it? No, because I'm too damn different. They won't even cast me as the character I really am. How crazy is that? And according to Fiona, the only other roles for me now are more freaks and outcasts. Four and a half months of fame, and I'm already washed up.

No matter what I do, no matter how hard I try, nothing ever turns out for me. I get close enough to taste it, to feel it on my tongue, but only one little bite. I never get the whole meal.

I'm so damn tired of being different I can barely think. So *what* if I have scars on my face? Why is that so damn important to everyone? Why is that all they ever see? In the end, it's always the only thing that matters. Why can't people ever just see *me*?

Now here's Russel, coming into my room, piling on the pity, saying he *understands* me. But he doesn't understand. He *can't* understand! He's never had to deal with the shit I have to deal with.

And he gets to be with Kevin, the love of his life, and they get to talk and laugh with each other on the phone every night before they go to bed. And when this trip is all over, Russel gets to go home to him, to the apartment where they live together, where they've built a home. They have a couch where they cuddle together when they watch TV, and a kitchen where they can make chocolate chip cookies and laugh about whether eating the dough raw will give them salmonella. And they have a new bed in their bedroom where they can have sex every night, real sex, the kind you have with someone who sees you as a sexual being—the kind of sex you have with someone you love.

But I'll go home alone. I'll *be* alone. I don't have any of what Russel has: not the apartment, not the cookie dough, not the sex. Why? Why couldn't I have that with Russel? We had that together once, but only for about five minutes, just a little taste of it. How come he gets to get the guy, the happy ending, but I never do?

Is this the real issue, the reason I'm suddenly so angry with Russel? Is it because he ultimately chose Kevin over me? Well, so what if it is? Russel *did* choose Kevin over me. Like Spencer chose to ghost me, like every guy always chooses someone else over me. They get the guy, and I don't, and that's all about my face too. Yet again, I'm too different.

"Otto, I'm sorry," Russel says. "That was stupid of me to say. I have no idea what you're going through. Hey, Julian said we could stay for the weekend, right? Well, why don't we get showered and go down to the French Quarter?"

As he's talking, I realize that this is about my face too. He's feeling *sorry* for me. Everyone feels sorry for me because they don't want to *be* me. They know how shitty it must be, and how lucky they are that they're not me, so they say whatever stupid thing they can think of to make me feel better. Or maybe it's to make themselves feel better. Either way, it doesn't ever mean anything because it's only words. Because I still don't get the part, and I still never get the guy.

"Gumbo!" Russel is saying, "You know, I don't think I've ever even *had* gumbo. What is it anyway? It's a kind of chowder, right? Anyway, we'll get some gumbo, and then maybe we can—"

"*Stop patronizing me!*" I say.

Suddenly I know the real reason I'm angry at Russel: because I love him and he doesn't love me back. It doesn't have anything to do with him. But I don't care. I'm still so mad.

"Stop feeling sorry for me!" I go on. "I'm so *tired* of everyone always feeling *sorry* for me!"

"Otto, I'm just trying to—"

"I don't need you to do *anything*, okay? Just leave me *alone!*"

Russel stands up from the bed, his back stiff. He's taller than I remember, or maybe it only looks that way because I'm still in bed.

He turns to face me. His face is flushed, and his whole body is tensed, like he's the one who has to restrain himself, to keep from saying what he really thinks. There's something else going on here, some more subtext I don't understand, but I don't care what it is. What does he have to be angry about? He's the one who ended up with the happy ending.

"Do you mean that?" he says to me, very quietly.

I think about that conversation I had with Mo where I said that being with Russel even though I couldn't be *with* him was better than the alternative—than being alone. But that doesn't feel true anymore.

So I say, "Yes!"

He says, "Maybe it's better if I catch a bus back to Los Angeles on my own."

I can tell he's expecting me to object, to beg him to stay, to say that I'm sorry for all the things I've already said. But I'm not sorry, so I don't. In fact, the last thing in the world I want right now is to have to spend another four days sharing every waking moment with Russel fucking Middlebrook.

"Take a plane," I say. "Send me the bill—I'll pay for your ticket. But yeah, I think maybe you should go."

CHAPTER FOURTEEN

I hear Russel moving around outside my door, gathering his things, but I still don't get up, not even to pee. I give him plenty of time to clear out.

My phone rings, and I see it's Fiona.

I'm hoping against hope that maybe she has some good news, so I answer. "Hey."

"What the hell is going on?" she says.

"Huh?" I say.

"You went to *New Orleans*? To audition for *Julian Lockwood*?"

"Well, yeah, but I didn't get the part."

"Trust me, I *know* you didn't get the part. You've also made me look like a complete idiot. I didn't know anything about any of this."

I'm in no mood to deal with her right now, but I say, "Well, I didn't know you didn't know. Greg said you did."

"Greg didn't tell me a thing! I was completely in the dark."

Now I'm confused. Why wouldn't Greg tell her? But then I remember how Fiona treated me that day in the office, and I can't help but wonder: Did he think Fiona wouldn't *let* me read for the part? But why?

"Well, can you ask him?" I say.

"Ask him yourself," Fiona says, "because I fired him."

"You fired him for almost getting me the lead in a great movie directed by Julian Lockwood?" I say, talking before thinking.

"You did *not* 'almost' get the part. You've wasted the time of everyone involved! And I could have told you that if you talked to *me*."

Really? I want to say. Because I'm staying in Julian Lockwood's house right now, and he sure didn't sound like I was wasting his time the day before. Part of me wishes he was still home, because I'd love to walk down the hallway and put him on the phone. Isn't there a movie where something like that happens, Woody Allen or something? If Russel was here, he would know.

Fiona doesn't say anything for a second.

"Otto..." she starts.

And I know exactly what she's going to say: something about how sad she is that I don't trust her judgment about my career, and that she doesn't feel that it's working out anymore.

Sure enough, she starts to say it, so I hang up on her.

I admit I'm curious to hear Greg's side of the story, but I don't have his cellphone number, so I can't call him. Instead, I finally go to the bathroom to pee, but I've waited too long. It takes forever to start, and it really hurts once I do. And even when I'm done, I still ache inside something bad, and I wonder if I somehow damaged myself.

I have no idea what I'm going to do next, not even if I'm going to take a shower. Do I drive back to Los Angeles by myself? I suddenly feel like an idiot for buying that expensive Mini-Cooper Convertible in the first place, especially since it now looks like my career is over and I'll probably need the money. Maybe I can sell it.

There are frilly things in the bathroom, colorful soaps and scented shampoos. Julian Lockwood has a wife or a daughter. But I'm too tired even to snoop in the medicine cabinet.

I finally realize that I'm hungry. Eating seems like something I can manage, something practical and distracting, so I put on some clothes and go down to the kitchen.

Julian Lockwood is sitting at the breakfast table reading his iPad.

"Oh," I say. "I didn't know you were here."

"Yes," he says. "But I have to go out again in a bit."

"Sorry," I say, but I'm not sure what I'm apologizing for. The fact that I haven't showered and probably stink? That's as good a reason as anything.

Julian Lockwood stands and goes to pour me a mug of coffee.

I nod him on. "Black."

As he pours, he says, "Where did Russel go?"

"He decided to fly back home," I say.

"By himself?"

"It's a long story."

Julian Lockwood hands me the coffee, then stares at me, and I'm not sure if he's expecting me to explain about Russel, that we've had a fight. If he's been home all morning, he probably heard something. But I don't say anything.

Finally, he says, "Have a seat. I'll make you some breakfast."

So I sit, and I know I should probably be impressed that Julian Lockwood, Oscar-winning director, is making me an omelet, but I'm not. I feel like this is the least he owes me.

As he cracks eggs into a bowl, he asks, "Tell me. Why did you decide to become an actor?"

So I tell him the story of my being in *King Lear* in high school. But this time I add, "That was the first time I ever felt like that, being part of something real and beautiful. But ever since then, all I've ever played is zombies and freaks, and a small role on a bad sitcom. So I guess that was also the *last* time I was part of something real and beautiful."

This last part sounds exactly as bitter as I intend.

"You want to hear something interesting about being a Brit in America?" he says.

"Why not?" I say.

"You can swear at people and they don't know you're swearing at them."

I stare at him skeptically.

"Seriously!" he says. "I do it all the time on the set. I'll call someone a bellend. Or a clunge. A twonk. Or a hobknocker, a munter, or a wankstain. I'm usually very serious, but they don't get it at all. Even if they understand I'm swearing, I'm doing it in an English accent, so they somehow think it's charming."

"Nice," I say, not even tempted to smile.

Julian Lockwood is finished with my omelet now. He slides it onto a plate, then adds some fruit salad from a container in the refrigerator—melon and pineapple, bright green and orange and yellow—and puts the plate in front of me.

"Just so you know," he says, "being a movie star isn't the same thing as being an actor. Not at all. The job of a movie star is to be famous. Acting is just the excuse we all use to fawn and obsess over them."

"I know that," I say like I think he thinks I'm stupid. Julian Lockwood may have won an Oscar, but I don't have a lot of patience with him right now.

"No, listen to me," he says, "I know a lot of movie stars, but I don't know a single one who's happy. No, wait, maybe one. Sandra Bullock. The first time I met her, I wondered if she wasn't a little soft in the head. Sometimes I wonder if I know *anyone* in Hollywood who's truly happy. Then again, why would we be? The pressure we're under is insane, and yet so much of 'success' is beyond our control. You think you can predict what movies are going to connect—everyone acts like you can. But you can't. No one ever knows. The audience is fickle. And no matter what you do, no matter how determined you are to do good work, to pick quality projects, there's always someone on your heels—someone newer and younger and better-look-ing."

"I know what you're doing," I say, interrupting.

"What am I doing?" he says.

"You're doing the whole thing about 'be careful what you wish for, it's never what you expect.' Of course it isn't. That's life. But that's still stupid advice. I *didn't* get what I wished for, and now I see I probably never will. I get that Hollywood is all a big game, but it's still the game I chose to spend my life playing, and I'm losing. Your telling me fame isn't what it's cracked up to be is like your saying to a homeless person, 'You really don't want this big house in the Garden District, it's a hassle having so many rooms to clean.'"

Julian Lockwood snorts. I know he knows I'm right.

But I keep talking. "Talking down success is so easy for you. You won an Oscar. 'Oh, woe is me, I'll never get to be on the top of the world again!' Please. Don't give me that bullshit about 'life is so much harder once you've tasted success.' You're on the very top of the world right now. You won the game. You might not get to be on top forever? Well, boo fucking hoo. If you can't appreciate what an incredible thing happened to you, that you were lucky enough to get something that most people can only dream of, well, that's almost too pathetic for words."

It all comes out of me without thinking, but I can't stop myself. And even after I've said it, I'm not ashamed or embarrassed. Because I still know I'm right.

Julian Lockwood stares at me, not blinking. He looks completely blank, like I've slapped him—like I've stunned him.

Then his face cracks a smile.

"I said before I know a lot of actors," he says, "but I'm not sure I know anyone like you."

"You said you know a lot of *movie stars*," I say. "But you also said that movie stars aren't the same thing as actors."

Now Julian Lockwood raises an eyebrow. I've officially impressed him—this time, I realize, because I'm not trying to.

At this, I can't help but spin a little fantasy in my head. Could I be impressing Julian Lockwood so much that he'd reconsider me for the part in *The Tulip Vase*? I know what he thinks about movie stars, the pressure they're under. So could this whole invitation to spend the night be some sort of an actual "character" audition—one that I'm killing at? If Russel were here, I know that's what he'd be thinking—that this is how it would turn out in a movie. But unlike Russel, I know that life is no movie. I know there's no chance I'm going to get the part in *The Tulip Vase*.

I start in on the omelet, and it's good. It's made with sharp cheddar cheese, and mushrooms, and onions, and also something I don't recognize, something salty.

Julian Lockwood watches me eat.

"You want me to give it to you straight?" he says.

"Why not?" I say, still not having any fucks left to give.

"The odds of someone like you becoming a movie star are ten million to one."

Now *I* raise an eyebrow. But I can't really disagree.

"Then again, the odds of *anyone* becoming a movie star are at least a million to one," he says. "Even Sandra Bullock. And when the odds are that long, is that really that big a difference between one million and ten?"

I smile, but not that broadly. As a struggling actor in Hollywood, I've heard stuff like this a lot.

"You didn't like the advice I gave you before..." he says.

"Not really," I say.

"Well, you were right, it was bad advice. Everything you said, you were right. When you're in Hollywood, I guess it's easy to lose perspective. But we're not in Hollywood anymore. So let me give you some different advice."

"Okay," I say, eating. I still can't figure out the extra ingredient in the omelet, and I want to ask Julian Lockwood, but I don't want to interrupt him. It's good—tangy.

"I heard you and Russel arguing this morning."

"I figured. Sorry about that." I'm tempted to point out that sounds really carry in this house of his, but he obviously already knows that.

"Did anyone tell you why I'm here this week?" Julian Lockwood says. "In New Orleans?"

"A family emergency," I say, suddenly feeling like an idiot that I'd never even bothered to ask him about that.

"My wife has Chronic Intrinsic Kidney Failure, and her dialysis is failing. We thought she was eligible for a transplant, but this week we learned that the chance of a successful surgery was deemed too low. She's moved into hospice—she's with her parents now. She's going to die."

"I'm so sorry," I say. "That's really terrible." My throat tightens, and I stop eating. I can't help but remember what Mo told me about her son dying. I feel bad for Julian Lockwood, but I also feel kind of stupid that I'd forgotten how much misery there is in the world—how I'm not the only person with problems.

"By the time I start shooting *The Tulip Vase*, my wife will be dead," Julian Lockwood says. "But in a way, that's kind of fitting. She wrote the screenplay."

"Your wife wrote...?"

He nods. "Under a pseudonym. That was the only way we could get the studio to take her seriously. And this is the story she wants me to tell. She wants people to know what's important in life. To recognize an opportunity when it comes, because it might not come again. Real life isn't like it is in the movies. It's tragedy, not comedy. We all know the real ending, the *only* ending, and it's not Happily Ever After."

"That's true," I say, nodding. I'm touched by all this, understanding why it's so important to Julian Lockwood that he's making this particular movie. But I'm already well aware that real life doesn't come with a happy ending. So I'm not sure what any of this has to do with me. My problem isn't my missing opportunities—it's that opportunities always seem to miss me.

"So your friend Russel is going home alone," Julian Lockwood says.

"Yeah," I say. I think: Why does he keep bringing up Russel? The less said about him, the better.

"What?" he says, because he senses there's something I'm not saying about Russel.

"Oh, Russel lives in a fantasy world."

"Does he?"

"Yeah. He's always got everything all worked out in his head, seeing things the way they are in the movies. But he doesn't see things as they really are. It's like you said. Life is tragedy, not comedy. Russel doesn't understand that."

"And you do?"

"I try to. That's why I like *The Tulip Vase* so much. It's different from other movies. It's about real life, about things as they really are."

I realize that my breakfast is growing cold, and I'm wondering if it's rude to start eating again, so soon after he was talking about his dying wife. I do, and Julian Lockwood watches me, but doesn't look shocked. At the same time, I finally realize what it is in the omelet, the thing I couldn't quite figure out.

"Kalamata olives," I say. "Chopped."

"What?" he says.

"In the omelet. I knew there was something, but couldn't figure out what it was. They're good."

Julian Lockwood ignores me. "Russel came to see me this morning. Before you were up."

"Really?" I say. I'm surprised, partly because Russel really isn't a morning person, but also because I didn't hear any of this, even tossing and turning in my bed.

"He asked me to reconsider casting you as the lead in the movie."

"Well, that's nice." I'm starting to realize I was pretty hard on Russel—too hard. I tell myself I need to send him a text to apologize. When I'm back in Los Angeles, I can take him out to a nice dinner.

"I told him it was out of my hands," Julian Lockwood goes on, "but then he immediately had another strategy. He had all these ideas for the script. He said I could add a new supporting character, one you could play. Zach's best friend, Emmett, who works part-time as a clown. But he's a sardonic sort, very blunt, never caring what people think about him. He always tells everyone the complete truth. Unfortunately, Zach doesn't listen until it's too late."

"The Fool," I say to myself.

"What's that?"

"It's the Fool character in *King Lear*."

Julian Lockwood thinks for a second, then nods. "Ah, yes, so Russel knows your story too, does he? Well, his ideas were excellent. They took the script to an interesting place."

The Emmett character *is* a good idea—I can already see how it would fit into the story. But I'm confused too. I didn't even know Russel had read the script. He must have done it last night after I left it down in the parlor.

Hope starts to well within me. If Julian Lockwood likes Russel's ideas so much, does that mean...?

"Alas, the studio would never go for it," he says. "I've been working on this project for four years now, and I know for a fact that the script is exactly as interesting as the studio is willing to go. And if I didn't already know that, then trying to cast you in the lead proved it."

"Oh," I say, my stomach sinking. Once again, it figures. But now I'm also feeling more and more stupid. Russel had done all this to help me, to try to get me the part, and I'd basically told him to get lost.

"In fact," Julian Lockwood says, "Russel's ideas were so impressive that I offered him a job on my next project—the one I'll hopefully be filming a few years from now. I wanted him to adapt a novel the studio has optioned for me."

"You did? What did he say?"

"He said he was very flattered, and really tempted, but he turned me down."

"Wait. What?" I say. Russel turned down a studio screenwriting job? "Why?"

"He said it wouldn't be fair to you. That the two of you had come all this way for you, and that if it ended up with *him* getting a job, not you, you'd be devastated. He said maybe we could talk about it again in a few months, if the job's still open, but it was too soon now."

Now it's not only my stomach that's sinking—it's my whole body, my chair and everything, right down into the floor. I know that Russel wants to be a screenwriter more than anything else in the world. And yet he'd turned down a dream screenwriting job with Julian Lockwood because he'd been worried how I would react, how I would feel. Is this what Julian Lockwood meant before when he'd implied I wasn't seeing things as they really are?

I think back on our road trip on the way to New Orleans, all the things Russel and I did to get here on time. At every point, each time I got discouraged, Russel was right there urging me onward. In fact, the whole idea of the trip had been Russel's in the first place. At one point, he'd even asked me why I'd wanted to become an actor, and he'd really *listened*—so much so that he was able to use the information when he pitched Julian Lockwood a rewrite of the script.

He'd been the best possible friend a person could have. Sure, maybe he'd pranced around the motel room in his underwear, but only because he didn't understand the effect it was having on me. And yeah, Russel had a great husband, the guy he'd ended up with rather than me, but that didn't mean he didn't love me too. He'd proven it to me over and over. But I'd missed it. I'd been so focused on the audition, and being lonely, that I hadn't thought about his feelings at all. In the end, he'd even turned down this huge opportunity, the thing he cared about most in the world, just to avoid hurting me.

Someone really was living in fantasy world, but it wasn't Russel. It was me.

I can't help but think: Have I always been this clueless? Ever since my accident, back when I was seven years old, I've spent a lot of time thinking about myself: how it sucks to be different, how unfair it is the way the world treats me. I guess I've sometimes forgotten that other people have their problems too—that not everything is perfect for them. Sometimes people's kids die in drug overdoses, or their wives have Chronic Intrinsic Kidney Failure. Sometimes people's screenwriting careers stay in the toilet even when their friend's acting careers start to take off.

And sometimes people have done their best to help me, not out of pity, but out of love.

I think about the Ana Ortiz Conundrum that Russel was talking about with Ernesto and Adriana. Is it better to be the supporting actor in a great story, or the star of a shitty one? I see now that's the wrong question. The right question, the only one that matters, is: Are you doing a good job or not? After all, there's another actor's expression: There are no small parts, only small people.

I realize I'm already the star of a story—my own—and I'm turning in a pretty miserable leading performance. But I'm also a supporting player in someone *else's* story: Russel's. And my performance there has been pretty lousy too. I sure as hell haven't been very supportive. Russel has supported me great, but I haven't done the same for him.

Am I even all that different from other people? That's what I've been telling myself my whole life, and sure, I have scars on my face and body—that does make me different in a way. But deep inside where it counts, am I just as selfish and self-centered as everyone else? I always tell myself that I'm totally different, but I start to wonder. Maybe I'm exactly the same.

And maybe that's not even true—maybe it's more self-serving nonsense. Maybe I *am* different deep inside where it counts, but in a bad way. Maybe I'm *more* selfish than other people. Would anyone else have been as much of a dick to Russel?

So this road trip has led to an unexpected realization after all, a twist ending. Russel had even said there was a Greek word for the moment when a person finally realizes the truth about himself. *Anagnorisis.* Anyway,

I'm definitely realizing I'm not the person I'd thought I was.

"But..." I start to say to Julian Lockwood.

"Don't be such a hobknocker!" he says suddenly. "Call Russel! Tell him you were wrong, and you're sorry. Is that explicit enough advice for you? Take the word of someone whose wife is dying. Russel may be the best friend you'll ever have, in Hollywood or any other town, and you were an absolute fool to let him leave."

I stand up from the table so fast the chair almost falls backward. But still I hesitate.

"*Go*, you little wankstain!" he says.

And so I do.

CHAPTER FIFTEEN

Out in the entryway by the flowers, I call Russel, but he doesn't pick up. I text him too, telling him how sorry I am, what an asshole I've been, but he doesn't answer.

Is he already on the plane back home? I try to calculate if he's had enough time to make it all the way to the airport and board. It doesn't seem like it, but I don't really know how far it is. I look up flights out of Louis Armstrong Airport, and there don't seem to be any direct ones to Los Angeles leaving soon, but who's to say he didn't hop on a connecting flight? If you're waiting around anyway, it makes as much sense to do it on a plane.

On the other hand, maybe he's still at the airport, but he's so pissed at me that he doesn't want to respond. If I was him, I wouldn't respond to me either.

Will he ever forgive me? That's the question. Or have I ruined the one true friendship I still have left now that my old friends are all jealous or resentful of me, and my *Hammered* friends are moving on to other projects?

I need to talk to him before he leaves. For some reason, this feels like the only chance I have to make things better between us. I'm certain that if he gets on that plane, if there are four whole days before I can talk to him and apologize in person, things will never be the same between us again. Four days is a lot of time to dwell on the fact that I've been such a dick.

I need to go to the airport.

I run upstairs and grab my things from the bedroom, cramming everything into the bag, then hurry for the door. As I'm fumbling down the stairs, I see Julian Lockwood standing in the doorway from the kitchen.

"Good luck," he says, and I nod.

I'm desperate to get going, to catch Russel before he leaves town, but I can't help stopping at the front door.

"Thanks," I say, and I really mean it.

"You said before that Russel doesn't see things as they really are?" Julian Lockwood says. "That he lives in a world of movies and fantasy?"

"Yeah. So?"

"So what's the point of life, anyway? Is it only to see things as they really are? Or is it also to be happy?"

I drive to the airport, desperate to get there before he leaves. Along the way, I check my phone, but Russel still hasn't texted me back.

I park my car in short-term parking and run into the terminal itself. That's when I realize that coming to the airport like this might not have been such a great idea, because there's no way I can get past security into the boarding areas, not unless I buy a ticket myself. I consider doing it anyway, but the lines at the counters are really long.

I jog along the ticket counters and kiosks, checking out all the lines, looking for Russel, but I don't see him anywhere.

Then I take the escalators up toward security. There are lines there too, and I look around for him, but I don't see him there either, or even in what I can see of the waiting area beyond.

The only other place he could be on this side of security is baggage claim. I don't know why he would be there, but I check it out anyway.

There are no flights that have come in recently, so the whole area is almost entirely deserted. Empty air swirls around me. It's air-conditioned and cold, and I shiver.

Then I realize I still haven't texted to tell Russel that I've come to the airport—that I'm *in* the airport.

Halfway through writing out the text, I look up.

Russel stands on the opposite side of the baggage claim, cargo shorts and everything.

He's far away, so I start walking toward him. He doesn't move. He stands there watching me, but I can't really blame him for that.

I start running. At least Russel doesn't leave. He stands there looking stiff.

Finally, I'm right in front of him. He's definitely not smiling, but he's not exactly frowning either.

"You're here!" I say, already a little out of breath. "You didn't get on the plane."

I think: Well, obviously. But even now, I can't read his expression.

"Julian told me everything," I say. "Russel, I'm sorry! You gave up a studio screenwriting gig? I can't believe you did that for me. But it's not only that. After every-thing you did to get me here on time, I turned around and treated you like I did. All I can say is that I've been in a strange place lately, for a lot of different reasons."

I stop, wondering if I should tell Russel the rest of it, how I still have feelings for him, and how I'm jealous of the way he is with Kevin—that he ended up with Kevin rather than me. But I quickly realize there's no point to it, that it'll only make Russel feel bad. It also feels a little like I'm making excuses, and I don't really have any good ones.

He doesn't say anything. He hasn't really moved since I spotted him from the other side of the baggage claim. It's like he's a cardboard cut-out—flat.

"Did you buy a ticket yet?" I ask. "Or even if you did, tear it up. Let's drive back to Los Angeles together. Okay?"

"I didn't buy a ticket," he says.

"Does that mean you want to drive back home with me?" I ask.

He shrugs—the slightest shrug in the history of the universe, but I'll take what I can get.

"Does that mean you forgive me?" I say.

And once again, he hesitates.

"Otto, you're one of my best friends," he says at last.

"You're one of mine too," I say immediately. "I'm not sure what I'd do without you in my life."

"But..." he says.

But?

"This morning I've been thinking about you," he says. "About our friendship."

I'm not sure I want to hear this, but I know I have to.

"And I'm not sure I've been entirely fair," he says.

197

"*You* haven't been fair?" I say, confused.

"I look at how the world treats you, and I feel bad. It makes me angry—at them and for you. On your behalf, I mean."

"And I appreciate that. I love that you have my back."

"I do, but that's not what I mean," Russel says. "Sometimes I think I make excuses for you."

"Excuses?"

"If anyone else treated me the way you did this morning, I'd be furious. The friendship might even be over."

I'm still confused by what he's saying, but now I'm scared too. What exactly is Russel telling me? He doesn't want to be my friend anymore?

"But with you," Russel goes on, "I'm tempted to say, 'Well, it's *Otto*. He's had a hard life. It's not *his* fault. Or even if it is, it's *understandable*.'" I hear him breathing through his nose, like he's still really angry. Then he says, "But it's *not* understandable. That's me making excuses for you. You were a real asshole to me this morning, especially all I've done for you this week, and I *am* furious."

"You are?" I say, cowering a little.

"That's what I mean when I say I haven't been fair to you. If two people are going to be friends, they need to treat each other like equals. One person can't make excuses for the other. If you're an asshole, I need be able to *say* that."

"And I was an asshole."

"You *were*."

"And I'm so, so sorry!" I say, tears rising in my eyes.

Russel ignores them. "You really disappointed me, and I need to be able to *tell* you that."

"I know. You do!"

I really do understand what Russel is saying: he's finally treating me like he would anyone else—no pity for me, no allowances because I'm "different." On one hand, I know I should be glad because this is what I've said I wanted my whole life. But at the same time, I'm realizing that it might mean he doesn't want to be around me anymore—that the tulip vase that is our friendship is too broken to ever be put back together.

Russel doesn't say anything for a second. He stares at me, thinking, his body as tight as a wire.

I hold my breath. A tear streaks down my face.

And then the wire releases, and Russel says, "And now that I've said it, and you've owned it, I can forgive you."

"Really?" I say, exhaling at last. I wipe my face.

He nods. "Otherwise *I* become the asshole. And it's still way too early in the day for that."

I'm still sort of crying, but now I laugh too. "Really? You mean we're still friends?"

"Of course we're still friends! How could we not be? I mean, you drove all the way out to the airport to stop me before I got on the plane."

"I did, didn't I?"

"And you said all the right things too. It was like a scene from a movie."

Now I hesitate. Is Russel testing me? Is this a reference to how I got so upset with him for mentioning movies in the bedroom this morning? If so, it's a pretty good test.

And I answer, "You're right. It's another movie cliché. Not necessarily a road trip movie cliché."

"Yeah, I know," Russel says, disappointed.

"But still. How many times have we seen that? The airport ending is definitely a *total* cliché." I'm laughing now, probably way overdoing it, but I'm so happy that Russel is forgiving me.

"Well," Russel says, "I may have helped things a bit."

"Helped things?"

"I was watching you on my phone."

That's when I remember we share an app where we can figure out where the other is. I've never really used it with Russel, but I feel stupid I didn't even remember it—that I didn't try to look him up before in order to track him down.

"I figured you were coming here to apologize," he goes on. "That's why I didn't buy a ticket. And..."

"What?" I say.

"Well, it might be why I waited until you were down here."

"In the baggage claim?"

He nods. "There were fewer people. And it made a better visual—you being on one side of the room, me being on the other."

"Wait," I say. "You've been watching me on your phone all this time, trying to make it so it would be more like some kind of movie cliché?"

"*Exactly!*" Russel says, as if the answer is incredibly obvious. "Are you kidding? I've waited my whole life to be in a scene like this! Tell me honestly: did anything crazy happen on the drive here? Did you get caught behind any parades? Oh! Or did you, like, run through a wedding party and steal the newlyweds' car?"

I laugh and shake my head like he's crazy. But I get serious again really fast.

"Thanks," I say.

"For what?" Russel says.

"Everything." I know he knows I'm talking about his not letting our friendship stay broken.

Russel nods, tapping the heel of his shoe on the floor a bit. "Well, it so happens I might know a thing or two about ignoring other people's feelings in a mad pursuit of a Hollywood dream."

"How so?"

"The way I treated Kevin when we first moved to Hollywood. You know most of the story, but not all of it. Don't worry, I'll fill you in on the rest some time. The point is, I was an asshole too. So I get it. I think there's something about Hollywood dreams that make people go a little crazy."

At the mention of Hollywood, I remember something. "Oh! You need to call Julian Lockwood." I fumble for my phone. "Right now. Wait, do we even have his number?"

"It's okay," Russel says calmly.

"No, it's not! You need to tell him you changed your mind, that you're taking his screenwriting gig. We'll drive over there right now." I turn in the direction of the short-term parking garage. "If he's not there, we can leave a note."

"Otto," Russel says, putting a hand on my wrist. "It's okay."

"It's not okay. You need too—"

"It's fine. We will. He'll take me back, I'm sure of it."

"*How* can you be so sure?"

"Are you kidding? There's no other way this story-arc can end. And in the meantime, this particular scene is over, so let's get the hell out of this stupid airport, okay?"

* * *

Out in the parking garage, my phone rings. It's Greg.

"Otto," he says, "I am so, so sorry."

Suddenly someone is apologizing to me. This is ironic.

"Why did you do it?" I say. That's what I really want to know, obviously.

"Because Fiona didn't think you were right for the part," he says. "She doesn't think you're right for *any* parts, except that damn *Nightmare on Elm Street* reboot. And can I just say? I knew she was wrong. I don't regret lying to her, but I shouldn't have lied to you."

I don't know what to say to this, how to process it.

"Are you okay?" Greg says. "I don't blame you for being mad."

This sounds a little bit like the conversation I had with Russel a few minutes earlier, but in reverse. And what's with all these people suddenly making these huge sacrifices for me? But things are definitely making more sense from Greg's end.

"I'm not mad," I say. "I'm actually really touched that you were willing to do something like that for me. You risked everything, and you got fired. Even though it turned out to be for nothing."

"It's not for nothing," he says. "Fiona fired me, but I've decided to start my own agency. And I still believe in you. I think you're incredibly talented, but it's not only that. I think the time is right for someone like you. I think the world *needs* someone like you. The world may not know it yet, but it does. And I'd love to be your agent, if you'll have me. I'm not trying to pat myself on the back, but doesn't this whole Julian Lockwood thing kinda prove I was right? You didn't get the part, but you almost did. So we'll get you another role. I found this part, I can find you another one. There was a time when Fiona really believed in you and your potential. But somewhere along the way, she lost faith. She gave up. Well, I won't give up. After this week, the things I heard them say about you, I believe in you more than ever."

Of course I'm going to sign with Greg as my agent. What idiot wouldn't? But I'm aware that he hasn't answered my question.

"You risked everything for me," I say. "You still haven't told me why." I know why Russel made the sacrifices he made: because he's my friend, and he's a really good guy. But I barely know Greg.

"I *did* tell you," Greg says. "Just now. Because I believe in you. Because I believe the world is ready for someone like you."

"That's the reason you want to be my agent. It's not the reason you risked everything."

Greg doesn't say anything for a second.

Then he says, "I might have feelings for you."

"Feelings?" I say.

"You know...romantic ones. Oh, hell, I've been interested in you for a long time! Happy?"

This is the last thing in the world I expect him to say, and I don't know how to respond. Greg has a thing for me? How did I get so lucky, having all these amazing people in my life? I'm starting to realize that maybe I'm not the terrible person I thought I was. If I was, would all these great people like me?

The more I think about it, the more I realize that Greg's feelings make sense. They explain the way he acted around me when I went into the office. The question is, why hadn't I ever noticed him? I'd always thought he was a nice guy, but I'd never considered him in a romantic way, or even that he might be gay. I can't help but think: Is it because he's big? Or Native? Or doesn't dress well? Talk about the irony of ironies. Did I never take Greg seriously because of the way he looks? Because he has more than one difference?

Now I'm back to feeling like a shitty person.

"Well?" Greg is saying. "Did you hear me?"

"I'm sorry," I say. "I definitely heard you, and I'm incredibly flattered."

"Flattered, but not interested."

"I didn't say that." After everything he's done for me, I'd also be an idiot not to give Greg a chance romantically. "But isn't it unethical for an agent to date a client?"

"It's not like I'm acting as your therapist."

"In that case," I say, "when I get back to Los Angeles, is there any chance you'd be willing to go out with me?"

"What do you *think*?" Greg says, and I smile.

We say goodbye, then I hang up the phone and look at Russel, who's been listening this whole time.

"It's not what you think," I say, even though it is probably exactly what Russel thinks. "It turns out he's had a bit of a crush on me for a while now."

"You are such a stud," he says, a sly smirk on his lips.

CHAPTER SIXTEEN

I'm in the spotlight. It's hot and bright, humming and vibrating all around me, like the light itself is alive.

I'm on a stage in a theater. There are people with me on that stage, co-actors in the play, and also other actors and stagehands, waiting in the wings. There are also people down in front of me too, seated in the audience.

But none of them are in the spotlight. They're off to one side or completely in the shadows.

I'm directly in that light. And it's exactly where I want to be.

It's April, six months after my road trip to New Orleans with Russel, and I'm appearing in a production of *King Lear* at the Pasadena Playhouse. It was a little bit like that time in high school when I'd happened to be passing by the auditorium where they were holding auditions. This time, I'd been scanning backstage.com, and I saw the audition notice. I realized how funny it was that my first acting experience, playing the Fool in *King Lear*, had been so positive, but I'd never played the part again. So I'd auditioned, and they'd cast me, but I think this time it was because they recognized me from *Hammered*. It wasn't until after we started rehearsal that the director realized how well I play the part, that my face really does fit the role.

Right now every single person in that theater is watching me. I can feel their eyes on me, bright and warm, even stronger than the spotlight.

At this point in the play, King Lear has been betrayed by his daughters, and he's been abandoned by his retinue of a hundred knights. The king is alone, except for Kent and his ever-faithful Fool. Kent asks the Fool where everyone else has gone.

As the Fool, I say, "That sir which serves and seeks for gain, and follows but for form, will pack when it begins to rain and leave thee in the storm."

Basically, the Fool is saying that everyone has left the king because his fortunes have fallen. They've realized that they can't gain anything more from him, so they've taken off.

"But I will tarry, the Fool will stay, and let the wise man fly," I go on. "The knave turns fool that runs away. The Fool no knave, perdie."

In other words, the Fool is too stupid to know when to leave. Or is he? The truth is, the foolish Fool is the only person brave enough to stay—the only person with any real loyalty to the king.

Kent asks me another question, and I answer, but then the play quickly moves on. The spotlight moves off me. I still have more lines later, but then the Fool disappears forever in the third act, and is never seen again, even though the play still has two more acts. It's something of a mystery what happens to him. At one point, the king does mention that his fool has been "hanged," but Shakespeare scholars aren't sure if that's supposed to be taken literally. But I think that whatever happens, it isn't the Fool's choice. The way I see it, he'd never voluntarily abandon the king.

Anyway, this is all okay. I'm only in the spotlight a little while, but I know my character makes a difference in the play. And I know I'm personally making an impression on the audience. It's at least as good as it was back in high school, maybe better, and even though I can't see the people outside of the light of the stage, I can *feel* them, and I sense them smiling at me even now.

Besides, I'll be in the spotlight again before too long. I'm sure of it.

After the show, the first non-cast-and-crew person I see is Greg, who meets me backstage. He's not supposed to be there, but he's an agent now, and he's used to giving off the sense that he is exactly where he's supposed to be. I may have also given him a few tips on dressing better, and now he's wearing Ballin Sharkskin pants and an untucked tailored button-down.

He gives me a big bear hug.

"You were fantastic!" he says, grinning. "A standing ovation, the day after opening night."

He's referring to the fact that almost every play gets a standing ovation on opening night, since the audience is mostly friends and family, and they've been given specific instructions to try and influence the critics. The real test of a play is on the nights that follow.

"Thanks," I say, blushing under my makeup.

Greg and I have been dating since the previous fall. Before our first date, I was worried that I wouldn't feel a spark, and it was definitely strange for a little while, being with a guy who's bigger than I am. Always before, the guys I'd been with have been about my own size. That's one of things I thought I *liked* about being gay—everyone being equal. But I've since discovered that equality doesn't have anything to do with size, and that, hey, there might be something kind of hot about the difference. As for the story behind his salmon tattoo, it turned out to be pretty interesting. Regarding the relationship, we're taking it slow, but it's going well so far.

Greg being my agent is something else I thought would be weird, but isn't. His agenting is nothing like Fiona's. I'll absolutely read for roles that take advantage of the fact that I have scars on my face—hey, my body really is my instrument—but Greg flatly turns down anything that he or I think is exploitative or retrograde, no matter how much money they offer. *People Magazine* never did put me on their 100 Most Beautiful People list, and so far I haven't landed any break-out roles, but I did do an episode of *Law & Order: Special Victims Unit*, and I'll be an injured marine on an upcoming episode of *Designated Survivor*. I even auditioned for *Game of Thrones*, which would have been a dream come true, but I didn't get the part. They loved my scars, but for some reason, they were on the wrong side of my face, which Greg and I both found almost too funny for words.

After that *Law & Order* episode aired, I was hoping to hear from Mo, but I haven't yet. I still think I will. I am in contact with Ernesto and Adriana. As for all the online harassment, I don't want to jinx myself, but it does sort of feel like it's tapered off, even if it's only because my career is a lot lower profile now.

I may not be a big star, but I'm a working actor doing interesting stuff, and that's more than most people in Hollywood can say.

Greg waits for me while I wash the makeup off my face and change, then we meet Russel and Kevin out in the lobby. I see them before they see me. They're standing together, loose and intimate, almost touching. Russel laughs like Kevin said the funniest thing in the world, and it's interesting seeing them alone like that, the two of them by themselves. They're one of those couples where they really *like* each other. I think that's one of the reasons why I always felt a little jealous—not only because Russel chose Kevin not me, but also because I always felt a little on the outside.

Kevin sees me first, and turns and says, "Bravo! Bravo!"

Russel steps forward and says, "You were fantastic! Exactly like I knew you would be." Russel's not a hugger, but he puts a hand on my arm and squeezes.

"Thanks," I say, grateful.

Russel and Kevin keep talking to me, telling me what they liked about the play and my performance, but they're also still standing together, shoulders touching.

Greg steps up next to me, and I feel his presence, big and comforting, and I relax, even as I realize that for the first time in a long time, I'm not jealous of Russel and Kevin, of what they have together, because now I have something similar with Greg.

"Are you guys up for getting something to eat?" I say to the others. "I'm always too nervous to eat before a show, and now I'm starving."

The four of us go to a restaurant on Pasadena's main drag—a really nice place with white tablecloths and fine china.

"It's funny," Kevin is saying, "but Shakespeare always kind of scares me."

Being an actor, I know a fair bit about Shakespeare, so it would be easy to make Kevin feel stupid for this. But I don't feel jealous of him anymore, so instead I say, "Oh, yeah, there's nothing quite as bad as bad Shakespeare. If the actors don't understand what they're saying, it's the worst."

"So bad Shakespeare is like bad Keanu Reeves?" Russel says.

"Hells to the yes," I say, laughing.

"But it was different with you," Kevin says. "Even when I didn't understand exactly what you were saying, I understood it because of the *way* you said it, and the way you moved your body."

"Thanks," I say, smiling. "It's crazy, isn't it? The idea we actors might actually know what we're doing?"

"What did Alfred Hitchcock say about actors?" Greg says. "That you're cattle?"

"Not that they're cattle," Russel says, "but that they should be *treated* like cattle. Which they should, but only when they're too stupid to understand what the writer is really doing." Then he adds with a smile and little mutter, "Which is most of the time."

"Maybe if you writers would write us something that isn't *crap*," I say.

"Yeah, bad movies are the fault of the *writer*, because everyone knows we writers have all the power in Hollywood!"

The whole table laughs, but especially Russel and me. We tease each other about stuff like this a lot.

Julian Lockwood's wife died two weeks after we met him in New Orleans, and Russel and I sent flowers. He really did get Russel that screenwriting job. A few months later, Russel turned in his first draft of the script, and supposedly the studio liked it. Russel made a lot of money—more than a hundred thousand dollars—and now he's hoping they'll keep him on a while for rewrites, and that maybe the movie will even be greenlit. Not long after he turned in his script, production started on *The Tulip Vase*, so Julian Lockwood has been too distracted to do anything else. But the three of us—Russel, Julian Lockwood, and I—had dinner together in West Hollywood once, and the most interesting part was all the people who stopped by to say hello. He introduced Russel and me to Angelina Jolie, who has *flawless* skin.

Working on that project with Julian Lockwood got Russel a lot of attention, and he signed with Greg too, who got him meetings with producers all over town. Russel has already had one of his spec scripts optioned, and now he's up for this writing project with Christian Bale. He even took a meeting for a movie about *Northstar*, one of the first openly gay superheroes ever to appear in mainstream comics, but it didn't seem like a serious gig, and it turned out the character is actually incredibly boring.

More than once, I've thought back on what Julian Lockwood said about the odds of any single person becoming a star in Hollywood being a million to one, and my personal odds being ten million to one. But Russel is already making it, and I'm more determined than ever to make it too.

I tell myself that success in Hollywood isn't about random chance—that it also has something to do with talent. With Russel, it sure does.

And on my bright and optimistic days? That's when I think maybe being different isn't a problem either. I think maybe it's exactly the thing I need to stand out.

The four of us stay and drink and eat for a long time—much later than we should, given that I have a matinee the following day. But we're all having a really good time, and it's one of those nights where you want to hold tight to it, not letting it slip away.

Finally, Russel says something about how the clock is striking midnight—even though it's already way past midnight—and Kevin is about to turn into a pumpkin. So the four of us stand and head for the door.

Out on the sidewalk, Greg says, "Hold on, I need to pee."

And Kevin says, "Yeah, I should go too."

"We'll get the cars," I say, and Russel and I go to give the tickets to the valet guys.

The two of us stand around waiting. It's late, but there's still a lot of traffic on East Colorado, and also noise from the other sidewalk restaurants. The night air smells like gardenias and car exhaust.

"You really were great tonight," Russel says.

"You know, I could hear you cheering," I say. "During the ovation? I heard you laughing too, earlier in the play."

This is true. His voice stood out from all the others, loud and clear.

"Well, of *course* you heard me laughing and cheering," Russel says. "Because I was laughing and cheering the *loudest*. I mean, duh."

Now I laugh.

Russel steps forward on the sidewalk, looking for our cars. "The day has finally come—I'm finally someone who uses valet parking!" he says. "I used to circle for thirty minutes looking for somewhere to park, all to save ten bucks."

I'm about to laugh again when a big black pickup truck zooms by right in front of Russel. It takes a second for it to register in my brain: the tinted windows, the jacked-up wheels.

Then I see the bumper sticker in back: *If Babies Had Guns, They Wouldn't Be Aborted!*

I can't believe it. It's really finally them. In Pasadena of all places.

But before I can even react, the truck is gone. I don't see how they could have seen us, not going that fast and with us standing in the shadows of the sidewalk. And would they recognize us anyway?

Russel turns to me, and our eyes meet, wide and white in the dark.

Then he bursts out laughing and says, "Oh, my God, that's perfect! I totally should have seen that coming!"

And I know exactly what he's talking about, how seeing that truck here tonight is somehow the real end to our road trip that started all those months ago. At the same time, I can't help but think about *King Lear* again, about the king who had everything, and then had nothing—except for his faithful Fool. Maybe having your sitcom canceled after one fifteen-episode season isn't the same thing as a king losing his kingdom, but somehow it *feels* the same, at least to me.

But it doesn't matter, because like King Lear, I still have one thing left too, and I know I always will: Russel Middlebrook, the world's greatest supporting player, and my own personal fool. He still dresses like an actual fool. Tonight it's a black belt with brown shoes. He often acts like a fool too, like with all his talk of those movie clichés.

He also speaks the truth. And in the end, he's always so incredibly loyal.

Part of me thinks I should still be scared of that big black pick-up truck, on the slight chance that maybe they did see us. Even if they didn't, that whole experience was downright terrifying. But I'm *not* scared, and I know it's all about Russel, how safe he makes me feel.

Now I'm bursting with emotion and energy, even more than I was on stage earlier tonight. Suddenly I want to tell Russel everything I'm thinking, everything I feel for him—not necessarily that I love him, but how much he means to me.

But before I can say anything, Kevin and Greg appear from out of the restaurant behind us, talking together. Right then, the two valet guys also drive up in our cars, one after the other. I still want to say something to Russel, but somehow I know the opportunity has passed.

We all say goodnight, and Kevin and Greg climb into the driver's seats of our different cars, and now it's just Russel and me alone out on the sidewalk.

As Russel starts for his car, I say to him, "Hey, you wanna catch a movie? Monday when the show is dark?"

He doesn't have to think about it at all. "Do you really need to ask?"

"With Kevin and Greg?"

He considers, then leans forward in a whisper. "Nah, let's lose the dead weight."

I smile, because it's exactly what I want him to say.

"I'll text you," I say.

"Not if I text you first!" he says, sliding into the car with Kevin.

And I climb into the car with Greg, and then we're heading down East Colorado, but I'm bursting with joy, as high as the stars, and I'm in the moment, riding it like a wave, feeling like it really will go on forever.

The story continues in:
Book 2 of The Otto Digmore Series,
coming soon!

BOOKS BY BRENT HARTINGER

The Otto Digmore Series
(Adult Books)
* *The Otto Digmore Difference* (Book 1)

Russel Middlebrook: The Futon Years
(Adult Books)
* *The Thing I Didn't Know I Didn't Know* (Book 1)
* *Barefoot in the City of Broken Dreams* (Book 2)
* *The Road to Amazing* (Book 3)

The Russel Middlebrook Series
(Young Adult Books)
* *Geography Club* (Book 1)
* *The Order of the Poison Oak* (Book 2)
* *Double Feature: Attack of the Soul-Sucking Brain Zombies/*
Bride of the Soul-Sucking Brain Zombies (Book 3)
* *The Elephant of Surprise* (Book 4)

Other Books
* *Three Truths and a Lie*
* *Grand & Humble*
* *Shadow Walkers*
* *Project Sweet Life*
* *The Last Chance Texaco*

ABOUT THE AUTHOR

Brent Hartinger is an author and screenwriter. The character of Otto Digmore first appeared in Brent's Lambda Award-winning young adult books, The Russel Middlebrook Series. The first book in that series, *Geography Club*, was adapted as a 2013 feature film co-starring Scott Bakula, and is now being developed as a television series.

Brent's other books include the gay teen mystery/thriller *Three Truths and a Lie*, which was nominated for an Edgar Award.

As a screenwriter, Brent has four new film projects currently in development.

In 1990, Brent helped found the world's third LGBT teen support group, in his hometown of Tacoma, Washington. In 2005, he co-founded the entertainment website AfterElton.com, which was sold to MTV/Viacom in 2006. He currently co-hosts a podcast called Media Carnivores from his home in Seattle, where he lives with his husband, writer Michael Jensen. Read more by and about Brent, or contact him at brenthartinger.com.

ACKNOWLEDGEMENTS

Thanks, as always, to my husband Michael Jensen and my agent Jennifer De Chiara, and also to this book's wonderfully picky editor, Jim Thomas.

Thanks to Philip Malaczewski for his series of great book jackets.

Early readers who generously contributed their time and extremely helpful opinions on this book include Jeff Adams, Flavio Boni, Tim Broeker, Brian Centrone, Casey Ellis (who helped with my King Lear references), Marco Guzman, Erik Hanberg, Will Haydon, Alan Hollis (who helped me with English slang), Brian Katcher, Jim Kruczinski, Stevie Jonak, Brad Lane, W.S. Long, Austin McCray, Walt Meyer, Lucas Orosco, Robin Reardon, Robert Rice (who gave me an actor's perspective), Richard Sakornbut, Tim Sandusty, Gregory Taylor, Christopher Udal, and Peter Wright.

5/2/19 - 5/9/19